Three Apples Fell From Heaven

Three Apples
Fell From Heaven

Micheline Aharonian Marcom

HarperCollins*Publishers*

HarperCollins*Publishers*
77–85 Fulham Palace Road,
Hammersmith, London W6 8JB

www.**fire**and**water**.com

Published by HarperCollins*Publishers* 2000
1 3 5 7 9 8 6 4 2

Copyright © Micheline Aharonian Marcom 2000

A catalogue record for this book is
available from the British Library

ISBN 0 00 226192 8

Set in Meridien by
Rowland Phototypesetting Ltd,
Bury St Edmunds, Suffolk

Printed and bound in Great Britain by
Clays Ltd, St Ives plc

For Nane and Dede

Նպտող Կատին Իրզա և Կատին Անմրման

Contents

viii

Not to have seen it yet inheriting it
Myung Mi Kim

At the edge of love, there we stand
Clarice Lispector

This Is the Story Rumour Writes

She writes it late at night, while you are dozing.

Rumour says things like, And so, and so

There was and

There was not

Rumour tells stories; this is the story she writes. Don't believe her: she's a liar of the first order. A mendacious tatterdemalion. A middle-of-the-night whisperer. She follows you and circles your head like stinging bees in late summer. She is disjointed, disorderly, malapropos. She begins in the middle, she stops and starts; she is a wanderer. When you look for her you cannot see her. Rumour says: Noah is my father and Japeth is my father and Haik walked down the slopes of Mount Ararat and squat under the cypresses to build a fire with still-green leaves. In 1915. Or in 520 BC, an inscription in stone of Darius I at Behistun. With breath there is always a beginning. A neonate lies on the sand; she is the founder of the nation. Rumour says, I am the founder of this nation. And so, and so

In a ditch, in a well, on the banks of the Euphrates

River, the trajectory of the river has been altered. In the desert, the Mesopotamian beetles drink blood and soup. There is a lake that overflows its bounds, trans-shapen by flesh. There are limestone houses and burned window frames, piles of manuscript, Gospel and gold buried in the garden. There are manifold dogs who have no need to scavenge. There are muted girls living in the haremlik of the jailmaster's house, in the kitchens and sowing the field. There is a sexton without a face, and his brother. There are caravans of invisible grave markers. There are new name places and streets, the heft of empty churches. The printing press is dismantled.

They are not the children of Japeth, the son to Noah, or Haik, who walked down the slopes of Mount Ararat and squat before the cypresses to build a fire with still green leaves. The eaves are empty. The hamam is closed. The bakers and the bootmakers uninvented. The furrier is still lamented in the coldest days of winter. The sweetmaker was spared for a hard candy. Do you miss them? Long for them?

Inside a ditch, in a filled well, up the cupboard staircase, beneath an indifferent oak, in a prison cell, by the Lake, on the stones, on the side of a road, in places that have no roads, by the lake, the attic, the wilderness, the hollowed heart that stinks, your mind: here. Their birth was in the time of fire, when God's wrath was immutable and adamantine, in the summer months of that year when all of the stories were destroyed and converged and the new story was pre-conceived – they were not themselves until then.

And so, and so

There are a surfeit of rumours. A surfeit of surfeit. Indigent rumours. Spiritual rumours. Fucking rumours.

2

Killer rumours. Bodies. Urine. Schools of orphans. Rumour often says, And so and so, if you insist too vehemently on any particular particular. She begins in the middle, she stops and starts; she is a wanderer. Rumour is an evanescent and mendacious tatterdemalion.

Rumour's covenant with her people: I shall not abandon you. A surfeit of surfeit for all time.

Don't believe it, she's a liar of the first order. A mendacious tatterdemalion.

An Omelette for Mama

She walks in the direction of the well now. It lies within plain sight further down the road. She doesn't look to it or breathe more quickly into the late-morning air, which is no longer still but bustling, although a bustling of a hollowed tempo. She speaks underneath her breath, pushes the words to the packed and uneven stones in front of her booted feet. She stares at the ground and at the tips of her shoes as they leave no dusty impressions. She whispers, Four eggs only, to no one in particular. She comes to the familiar wooden awning, to the Armenian bakery, and she turns right, down a small unpaved street, pushing the words out breathlessly, silently now, so as not to call attention to the idiom which could in these days attract more than a slap to the head or a rough cane blow. She has turned away from the quarter's well. There are no longer any dogs lingering outside the bakery door, she thinks, as she makes her way to the central market and the egg-seller's stall.

It is then that she begins to count the number of eggs she will purchase more slowly. One. Two. Three.

She makes the calculations in her head as a small child would with different combinations of numbers to reach the four: two and two, and two from six. She decides she would rather run than walk down the small alleyway where she has turned; she then imagines herself running, her hair coming loose from its plait, uncovering itself from the black veil which covers her today like a dark shroud. Closely behind this picture of flying braids and cooler air is another picture, quite suddenly, as she knew it would be, as it has been for weeks now, voraciously waiting: the black mole before her, the protruding blanched belly. The pot-belly baker and his mole-marked wife are like a sharp stone in her mind.

As she continues walking on the dull marble earth, she sees the hoary mole on Eghis Hanim's left cheek below her lower eyelashes; a protuberance of discoloured dark skin rises above the woman's pale flesh, pushing her left eye upward and making it smaller. It was a mole that became offended if you forgot to close the door to the bakery gently.

Children! Eghis Hanim would scream. We are more civilized than those dogs, no? Even if surrounded by them.

It is ugly like sin, Anaguil and her neighbourhood friends used to laugh among themselves.

Haigan would say, It's because that 'black doo' pulls all the goodness away from her heart.

She's a she-devil! Rachel would say.

A witch.

Anaguil would hunch her back and squint her left eye, pull her mouth and say, Eh, you stupid girls, don't you know how to close doors like Christian ladies? Whereupon all three childhood friends, friends from birth or close to it, would fall onto the garden grasses, laughing and rolling and holding their bellies.

Today the mole cannot be pushed out by numbers or calculations. One, and the mole appears; two, and then Eghis Hanim's big nose like a brass pitcher; three, and suddenly her coiled coiffure like a thick skein of dyed black wool. Eghis Hanim screaming at four, her hair (what few patches remained after her own fierce hands had ripped and torn it at the roots) flying like a maddened burning bush – the blood speckles were like field poppies, dull and invisible on the black shawl, in contrast to their flow and relief on her fair skin. Running, Eghis Hanim screamed not about doors or draughts or lazy girls. She clapped her hands and she sang and she danced, and she left her unbound locks strewn in the mud and in the vacant doorways.

And in the blue ashes of the vanishing world, she also vanished, Anaguil thinks. The blood from her scalp like the rose bush trickled down, like tears or dew or spittle, like the resin from a fir tree, onto the blue canopy of heaven which no longer is above our covered heads but lies below these booted feet.

Eghis Hanim screamed, I'll stuff my husband's head full of cabbage leaves! That's what you do with an undeliverable parcel.

Then the black mole gives way to the centre well and the aged oak trees and the tight red rose bush buds, and so Anaguil begins to count again. Quickly. Her feet imitate the beat of the numbers, almost at a run now, One, one, one, one. She does not count beyond one, just *one* because she understands that in between the numbers her own vile rememberings creep in like ugly desert beetles and that once she sees Eghis Hanim's moled countenance she sees the

6

stamp-seller with a polio limp and then the fat silk merchant Bakrat Gregorian and then the coin-seller who bought his two gold teeth in America. Then the orchard plums and yellow and red and purple and green grapes, and her sweetest uncle, Amo Berj, who said, We did not prepare ourselves adequately. And then and then: Baba. And then *one* as she comes upon the wooden stall of the egg-seller and slowly dips her hands into the folds of her çarsaf. With her right hand she touches the dull paras in her pocket; she clenches the coins. *One.*

Some eggs please, effendi.

And Eghis Hanim still echoes in the unspeakable noise of her mind, of the bazaar: *Cabbage leaves, cabbage leaves – they're so lovely with a severed skullcap! La-di-da.* Her mind like a book, she shuts it tightly and looks outside of her eyes to the old Turkish man before her and to the small mound of fresh hen eggs. She drops her gaze to the ground. A goodgirl.

Khalil Agha, the egg-seller, looks at the unchaperoned young girl standing quietly before him, her head bent and her hands tucked into her çarsaf.

How many eggs you need, girly?

Anaguil pulls her left hand from the inside of the floor-length veil and raises four fingers to the egg-seller's eyelevel.

Four eggs? You want *four* eggs, eh?

Khalil Agha stares at Anaguil's bent head and knows that since the war began seven months ago even small treasures can bring a profit.

The price is fifteen paras per egg. Prices have gone up today; these are difficult times. He smiles broadly, showing a missing incisor and a front tooth edged in black.

Anaguil stares intently at the packed dirt. She shakes her head. Ten paras, I have only ten.

Khalil Agha smacks his lips together, making a sucking sound.

They're not paying you too well, eh?

Anaguil presses the coins she is holding in her right hand into an even tighter fist.

Well, girly, for that I can give you one egg. A bargain for a sweetplum like you.

Anaguil thinks of the word one – oneegg – and she wonders if her thoughts have brought this moment into being; her thinking on *one* making it the only possible number. She removes her clenched hand from the çarsaf and stretches it toward the egg-seller; she opens her right hand, revealing a score of indentations left by the coins. The red crescents are relief for the ten paras in her palm.

Khalil Agha reaches across the table to take the currency. As he begins to remove the coins from her hand, he runs his fingers down the centre of her palm. He slowly glides his fingers along each of the red moons and when finished reaches to her wrist and then underneath the çarsaf. His hand skims her forearm.

Cacudes, Anaguil thinks, as she glares at the white pebbles lying next to her feet. When Khalil Agha squeezes her elbow through the cloth of the dress she wears beneath the veil, she clenches her hand again.

I do have discounts, cutie.

Anaguil shakes her head three times in the negative and notices in that moment how her hands perspire; she smells the bitter residue of the coins in the sweat of her palms.

No? No? Take your egg then, little-whore, he says, removing the coins from her hand. Even little-whores shouldn't come to the marketplace by themselves.

Anaguil receives the egg he hands her into the linen square she has brought from home. She carefully folds the cloth around the egg and for each fold of fabric she utters one syllable: I-shit-in-your-mouth: cacudes. The egg-seller's gaze is drawn towards her bitten fingers where only small stubs of fingernail remain. Anaguil turns away from the egg-seller's stall and she feels how the back of her dress now sticks to her skin; her hands tremble as she begins walking. It was worth it, she thinks, it was worth going to the market alone and buying from the son of an ass. The boys are at home safe with Mama, and I have done something I never expected. She disregards the burning feeling in her belly as she begins the walk home. She presses her thighs tightly together and ignores the need to relieve herself.

She passes the idle bootmaker's corner and the rows and rows of shuttered shopfronts as she winds out of the market. On another corner she passes the knife-makers' stalls. Anaguil smells the horns of goat in the high heat of the Turkish knifemakers' shops. The odours drift onto the morning air and into the mouth like bone, as the knifemakers melt and shape the cartilage and mineral life into handles and blades for cutting and slicing and killing. She hears in the distance the high-pitched call of the muezzin for the mid-morning prayer; it is a voice she has heard five times a day since the day of her birth and the sound is familiar, like skin.

Anaguil very deliberately moves her thoughts to her feet again, to each step that she is taking and to each step that she is about to take: one booted foot then another on hard-packed dirt, past discarded apple core,

9

spittle, dog shit; another booted foot, the toe scratched and worn as it veers onto the stone of the main road. She turns left, passing the closed bakery, passing the empty space where further down the road the well lies, and she heads towards home.

An omelette is what Mama needs, she whispers. An omelette with green onions. It will ease her spirits. In the summer we have always eaten them.

The wind has picked up since she left the house one half-hour ago. A tall cypress leans into the invisible force. Tall cypresses remind her of burial grounds, water, the colour of death.

Sargis Becomes a Writer

Dressed like a woman, can you imagine it? And sitting here in the pitchblack darkness like some mewling schoolgirl. My mother sneaks in dolma and cheese and pieces of fresh fruit and small strips of succulent lamb when she can get it. What I would give for the simple and unfettered pleasure of standing in the garden and tipping my head to the sun and the sky, of talking with the neighbour's beautiful girl Koharig in front of the white lilies, and lazily smoking a cigarette. I would even climb the mulberry tree like I did as a boy; I would shake the branches so that Mairig and my sisters-in-law could catch the berries in the blanket they'd hold like a fisherman's net below me. The red fruit would rain down in one thunderous catch and we'd laugh, thinking of the delicious fruit spreads Mama would make. I would feel the slight wind on my cheeks from the rush I had created in the branches. I would breathe the blue-white in the sky, the crimson in the berries, green on the leaves and the grey of the tree bark. My cheeks would puff up like a rodent's with the fruit I would pilfer. Mairig says these cheeks

11

are beginning to look sallow, and that I'm not eating enough. Bollocks, I say. But I seem to have lost my big appetite.

When we saw Professor Najarian running in the street like a crazy man, Mairig, who has always been my clever mama, grabbed me by the collar and pulled me up the hidden ladder into the attic saying, Not my boy, they will not touch my youngest boy. Later that evening she brought my books and some wax candles into this dark hole. The following week she pulled off my suit jacket and pants as if I were a two-year-old child, and while I was spitting and hawing, pulled an old woman's mu-mu over my head. Now I look like an old Christian village woman. Mairig wanted to go as far as rubbing ash into my cheeks but I said, Enough, they can't even see my face with this headscarf!

If it hadn't been for Professor Najarian, I probably would have resisted my little mama. I don't think I will ever erase the last image of the professor from my memory. Perhaps I will never again see him as he was when he lectured to us at the Euphrates College, with his stern voice and drooping dark eyes, his large waxed moustache that stretched from jowl to jowl and curled delicately at each end like a girl's hair ribbon. Now when I think of our esteemed professor I can only see him dancing naked in the streets between his wife and three daughters. No matter how hard I try to re-enact his lectures on poetry and philology, I can only hear him singing and babbling like a lunatic. This too feels like a betrayal.

The day he was released from prison after a fortnight's stay, we all stood behind our shuttered windows and peered surreptitiously through small cracks into the almost empty street. From our street windows we had a direct view of the professor's house and so we watched how the gendarmes dumped him in chains in a heap at his doorstep. He and Mussig Agha (whose wife had been able to prove her husband was an Assyrian by birth) were the only two men released from the group of detained intellectuals and prominent businessmen arrested in March. Each of the others had passed beneath our windows at night in an old wooden cart; their corpses were dumped at the edge of town in a large and unmarked hole. Ignominious death. Urine on their faces. Beard and chest hairs plucked out. Fingernails and toenails removed. The look of death on their faces, frozen. Ears disjoined and bloodied clothing sent to the wives as mementoes. Eyeballs for afternoon tea. Severed skullcaps.

The professor was the only one to leave the konak with his extremities intact. Yet the damage had been done. Who could recognize the gibbering and drooling naked old man with shit pressed into his hair and groin and filling the cracks of his arse? The man who yelled at the top of his lungs like a stuck sheep while his wife, Digin Hassig, and three daughters tried to cover him with a blanket and escort him back into his home?

The world is a pile of dung and a crock, la-la, and a crock, la-la, of hor-sees' doo! the professor sang, and wiggled his hips, and then began to yowl like a feral cat while his wife and daughters tried to hold on to his twitching arms. The Turks stood laughing a few feet away as he was escorted inside; it must have been better entertainment for the gendarmes than even the previous weeks' fun. As Digin Hassig tried to close the door, the professor stretched his neck and turned his head to the sky and cried, Where will the next tête-à-tête be, O Lord? And one of the laughing gendarmes yelled out, Don't worry, Professor, we'll invite you to another party very soon! The professor twisted his neck to look behind him at the police and yelled back, Thank you, thank you, effendi! If his hands had been free, perhaps he would have waved to them gaily.

Once Mussig Agha was back in his home the gossip spread throughout the quarter about the torture of the men. Word travelled of how the professor had been chained on a high ledge in the room where the gendarmes practised their black art. He had been the chosen one. The professor witnessed the beatings and slashings of his friends and colleagues, he felt the splattering of their blood when it arced steeply, and he heard their continual screams for mercy. He was told the same would happen to him unless he confessed where the arms were hidden.

Mussig Agha says the professor saw everything. Day and night for days and days. Mussig Agha says they didn't let him sleep.

Toward the end of the first week the professor began to rub himself in his excrement (they left him to urinate and defecate on himself) with the aid of his unbound feet, and to laugh like a demented child. After that the gendarmes loosed him and let him roam the prison grounds freely – he amused and entertained the working men. He performed his assigned duties. He folded the soiled clothing carefully so that it would arrive in a neat bundle to the owner's family.

In the days after the professor was released, the late nights became unbearable for the inhabitants on our block. I could barely see him from my hiding place, from the tiny attic window which gave on to the street. Whether or not I saw him, I always heard his screeching cries as he ran through the dark night, yelling at the top of his lungs, Somebody stop them! They're doing it again! They're doing it again! – after which he laughed uncontrollably.

For eleven days after his liberation the macabre scene was repeated. Mairig said the neighbours listened in fear but did nothing, only watched through their curtains as the professor ran naked up and down the street while his wife and three daughters trailed after him with a large coverlet. On the twelfth night I waited for him patiently as I had on previous days; I do not sleep until dawn in the attic. The streets were quiet all night, and for the first time in days I felt relieved and even a bit hopeful by morning: perhaps the man was regaining his senses.

Later that morning Mairig told me that the professor's heart had stopped.

Everyone is thankful that his suffering has ended, she told me.

Witnessing our brilliant professor lose his mind has caused me the worst kind of grief.

He received a proper burial in the cemetery. He lies in a marked grave and his face, they say, bore a stiff smile.

I've been in the attic twenty days. The gendarmes have begun to search the houses throughout the Armenian quarter more frequently; they still say they are looking for illegal arms caches. That is the reason they give for everything – for arresting and torturing the prominent teachers and businessmen of Kharphert, for coming into our homes uninvited. The town crier announces on each street corner that the Infidel is planning a *coup d'état*! We ask ourselves: for Godsakes, what 'caches' and armed rebellions are these shit-in-the-mouths talking about?

Some of the families in the quarter are now desperately trying to purchase arms to turn in to the Government: it has been said that if we turn nothing in they will know we are hiding something. But Mairig is clever: I don't trust those dogs. Do they think we are imbeciles? Stupid bleating sheep? And disregarding the orders, she dismantled the antique pistol Hayrig had sometimes used for hunting quail, burned its handle in the fire, and buried the metal pieces in the cellar.

When Hayrig was alive and the centuries' old rules still applied, he always paid the fee to keep his sons out of the army. Now even gold does not seem to help. The officials accept the payment, smile reassuringly, and then send the gendarmes to round up the men while the women wave the papers futilely and protest as ineffectually as squawking birds: Here it is, effendi. Look, effendi, my husband's pardon. We paid, sir. What are you doing, effendi! By God, we paid. Look here at this paper! Here!

My older brothers worried about the changing climate in town, but wouldn't listen to Mairig's pleading that they also hide in women's clothes.

I will never don a woman's habit. Things will settle down, Mama, my brother Melkon said, you'll see.

When the call came for Armenian men between the ages of eighteen and twenty-five to report to the commissary, Mairig came up to the attic to inform me.

They're taking the young men now. But you are not a boy for this war, son. I showed them your papers for advanced study in the capital. I told them you'd departed weeks ago for Constantinople.

As the days passed I tried to do my reading and keep up with the course work from the college. I wanted to be prepared to take my exams in autumn so that I could later take up my extended course of study in the capital as planned.

Three days ago the decree came from Constantinople, demanding that all Armenian males between thirteen and seventy report to the commissary. Already the gossip has been circulating about the earlier recruits digging the trenches for their own burial pits. Last night the police began to break into the homes and drag men out forcibly. From my perch in the attic I heard the cries of the women throughout the quarter.

He has done nothing!

What are you doing?

Let him go!

Dear God, have mercy upon us.

I dared not look through my small window for fear someone would see me. I used the brass bowl again and again to relieve my bowels. Mairig climbed quickly to the attic at 4 a.m. crying, Sargis! Sargis! They've taken your brothers. They're taking all of the men now. And she was at once assailed by the foul stench in the small space. I looked down at her as she stood on the top rung of the ladder.

Ah no, Mama, I said, don't come in now. And I cried quietly, as if I were a schoolgirl. The following day it was quiet in the quarter. Quiet as the grave, as the old people say here.

With the long days in the attic, as I tired from the reading by candlelight, I began to think of writing. It was as if my hands wanted to record of their own volition. I began:

There is nothing of more importance to an Armenian than his books. For we understand that we have survived in this hostile land for thousands of years because of three things: our language, our faith, and our texts. And it is in our texts that our language and our faith have been preserved. The people know that Armenia has been preserved in the books and that the books have been testament of our people.

We are a culture that bases our existence on the Book. Let us recall that our first work of Armenian literature was, after all, the translation of the most holy of texts: the Gospel. This is what is offered to the people in our liturgy: the word of God: sepculum gloriae Dei. The book is sacred, thus the holy book is never directly touched, we do not sully it with our stained hands.

Dammit. I sound worse than a pompous cleric.

For the Armenian, the book is more precious than wife or mother. The book is the symbol of our preservation as a people under horrible domination.

Shittyshit bollocks.

Eh, Mama? Yes, I hear you. Yes, I would like some tahn with lunch.

Hamam

Anaguil enters the kitchen quietly and remembers that today they will go to the hamam. She hates the baths now, the clay and grit and hot air, the light-light gossip, like buttercream. The Kurdish serving girl, Kara, is seated on a stool at the table, sifting through the lentils for small rocks and debris. Her hands are red and chapped; her brown hair falls to her waist in one loosely bound plait. She talks beneath her breath and, upon hearing Anaguil, raises her head and smiles slightly. She lifts her arm and waves a hand up and down, like a clumsy bird slipping from level to level.

Good day, Fatma Hanim. You bring thisummmthing for bulgur?

Kara is still learning her Turkish in the kitchen. She uses her hands and the space around them to communicate. *This* is often substituted for *that* and *that-one-over-there* in the sometimes confusing demonstration and demarcation of space and things.

Anaguil goes to the cupboard and opens it and retrieves a small bowl.

Fatma Hanim, no! Big one!

19

Anaguil takes down the bowl and then turns back to Kara to retrieve the sack of bulgur; she sees the servant girl looking at her strangely. Kara spreads her arms out wide into an arc.

Fatma Hanim, Fatma Hanim, you hear? she says, pointing at her ears.

Anaguil hears the girl and the name and she sees the sullen gesturing hands and stares into Kara's face, wondering if the moon-facial features of a girl can reveal a piece of her spirit.

Yes, Kara. Fatma Hanim will get the larger serving bowl.

She goes to the cupboard and she puts back the smaller bowl in exchange for the larger blue enamel one. Anaguil fills the bowl with five handfuls of bulgur, careful not to spill even a grain as she knows they are nearing the end of their store. She passes by the servant girl in search of the water to pour over the coarse wheat so that it may soak; she retrieves the brass water pitcher from the floor and she lifts it up heavily, expecting the full weight of the water in counterbalance. The pitcher flies over her head like a metal whip. It hits the ground near Kara's bare feet, and the girl looks up startled.

Bring water, Fatma Hanim? she laughs.

Anaguil looks at her stubbed fingers and thinks how in one year and nine months her fingernails have still not fully returned. She wonders if they'll ever come back between the pinkish folds of skin in neat squares. She bites at the hard edges of her index finger, then brushes by Kara and picks up the brass pitcher, placing it on the wooden table by the servant's busy sifting hands. She leaves the kitchen and goes in search of her sister, Nevart. There are no windows in the small

20

kitchen and she can no longer bear rooms without windows for long.

Anaguil attributes her difficulty in hearing to the music playing in her head much of the time. She can hear like a crystal brook the dumbeg and the 'ud or the voice of the troubadour: If I were close to you/I would give you a kiss/Then surrender my life to you. It is difficult to stop listening and to break up a perfect lovesong in order to respond to a *How is Fatma Hanim today?* or to a request for water. But Anaguil is disciplined and she does not always allow herself to follow the scales and 10/8 metre. Only in the evenings as they sit around the tonnir will she let the music come loudly and quietly, her body still except for the fluttering hands at her breastbone, which tap and scratch the rhythm, which feel the gold cross that is no longer there, feel its burn into skin just as she can feel the burn of the coals of the hot tonnir with her feet tucked tightly underneath the blankets, her toes extended towards the warmth of the round heater that the women sit around on cold nights. Anaguil's hands play with the emblazoned emblem on her chest. The fingers are not still. They are like small birds in a music box. Sometimes the relief of the melodies upon her skin is with her for days: a burn, a tiny nest, a swollen rose-brown kiss.

In the hallway, Anaguil's feet drag, interrupting sweet melody and her quest for Nevart. She looks down to see how the worn leather of her left boot has finally torn from the sole. There is a gaping hole, a hole from nowhere she thinks, unexpected. Her toes slip out of the shoe and she falls down in the hallway, halfway between the kitchen and the salon. She hits her head upon the stone floor. There is also a falling down inside of her, unexpected, that momentarily does not contain itself; it is louder than the music. She laughs. All of this is unwitnessable, silent, until it breaks outside of her a little, and then a little bit more; bit by bit the laughs erupt like unstoppable streams from Anaguil's throat, her tongue, her teeth, her cracked lips. She laughs out loud. And then Anaguil notices the laughter as a foreign thing, as she herself has become to her self and to her town; she realizes that it has been one year and nine months since laughter, and she laughs again, she giggles like a wild child. It is audible. Melodious.

I'm a goodgirl. And Anaguil bursts out wildly, all of the steam and ooze of living pushing forth in her effusion of mirth, all of the sticky shit. Goodgirl goodgirl goodgirl, how will you fix your boots? And a pitch-dark sound issues forth from her belly, echoing in the chamber and throughout the three-storey house, causing Kara to stall her sifting for stones and Gülhan Hanim to look up from her sewing and Nevart and Ahmet in the garden to giggle also.

There are only dead bootmakers in Kharphert nowadays.

They assemble in the salon at one o'clock: Gülhan Hanim, Anaguil, Nevart and Ahmet. Baby Bülent is only two years old and so he will remain behind with Kara. For Ahmet and Nevart the baths are part biweekly discomfort and part carnival. For Anaguil it is impossible not to notice how her shoulders stiffen and her arms lock during the hours they spend there. For Gülhan Hanim it is expected that they will go and that they will be clean according to the oldest traditions.

Let's go then, eh, children? Gülhan Hanim says. Fatma, did you bring the sandals and towels?

Anaguil nods her head. She carries a linen sack full of bathing sandals, cotton sheaths and towels bought in Sivas. She carries two oranges and some tourshi. The wooden sandals bite into her hipbones as she walks, jarring her and pleasing her also. They go through the back door of the house and into the walled garden where they find their escort, the old servant Ismet. They will take the shorter route through the back gate of the garden, onto the narrow alleyway heading south towards the ancient hamam.

As she is walking, as Ismet is leading the way and Nevart and Ahmet are swinging Gülhan Hanim's hands, Anaguil thinks of what she saved. Eclectic items: Mama's blue flowered scarf; Baba's American pocket watch, his gold Waltham with the Roman numerals; a burgundy and cream kilim Nene Heripsime wove in the late winter evenings in front of the tonnir; the 1912 family photograph; the small carved Bible no bigger than her hand; and Mama's wooden bath sandals, carved from oak, inlaid with mother-of-pearl.

They were the wooden sandals her mother had worn each time they went to the baths in all of the years that Anaguil could still remember. They were refined bath sandals: a small wooden slab the size of a woman's foot, cut into the shape of a sinuous vase and inlaid with dozens of iridescent triangles creating flowers and borders. Each slab was nailed to two straight wooden supports, like miniature stilts. The wooden supports measured the length of a hand so that the women had to walk slowly and carefully in their high-heeled sandals. The water flowed beneath

23

their sandalled feet, as if through tunnels, almost unobstructed.

Anaguil hokees, you have brought Mama's sandals? her mother would ask as they all stood in the garden waiting. Her brothers would come to the baths also: Nishan, Jirair and Stepan, before blue-eyed Nevart was born. And then, as well as now, Anaguil would carry the cloth bag of sandals and towels for everyone. Her mother would laugh at the boys' sour faces as they walked down the dirt and stone roads to the bath-house. Anaguil would laugh also, thinking not how she hated but how she loved the hours they spent in the hamam every other week; in the world of women and loosened flesh and breasts and bellies of every kind and shape and shade, and sweet or sour gossiping, familiar as hot tea and warmed flat bread.

Gülhan Hanim points to the trees above Nevart and Ahmet's heads. The garden is a spectacle in the spring-time; pay close attention to the mulberry tree, it is the harbinger of the season, she tells them.

For Anaguil the tree is more than springtime, it is the town when it was itself: Kharphert for more than one thousand years. The deep red toffee they made from the tree's fruit, wrapped in paper and brushed with powdered flour. Sweetness on the tongue.

They walk to the bathhouse in under a quarter of an hour. Ismet goes across the street to wait for them in the coffee-house. Gülhan Hanim pays for the chil-dren and for Anaguil and they enter through the heavy wooden door. Up on the balcony Hamamji-Khatoon, the bath attendant, stares at the group and then gives the nod: it is OK to enter with the boy, he is not too old yet to be allowed into the private world of women. With the flick of her chin, Hamamji-Khatoon directs the family to an available compartment in the middle of a large dressing area. They walk around a noisy fountain shooting up water from its circular base. Goldfish swim in concentric circles in the white waters.

The fountain makes a continuous and melodious accompaniment to their undressing. Gülhan Hanim removes Ahmet's boots and trousers and then kisses the boy once on each cheek as she removes his shirt and undergarments. Anaguil kneels and removes Nevart's black scuffed boots, wool socks and yellow dress. When the children are naked, the two women undress. Anaguil hands Gülhan Hanim her cotton dressing robe, which the mother then ties around her chest; Anaguil dons her own robe after she has removed her dress and undergarments. She puts her feet into her plain wooden sandals and places all of the family's clothes and shoes onto the provided copper pan. Gülhan Hanim walks steadily in her gold tasselled bath sandals to the second door.

Walk slowly, children.

Gülhan Hanim's large breasts sway beneath the bath sheath with each careful stride; her mother's milk is still heavy with her.

The family approaches the second wooden door leading to the inner chamber. The door opens and steam rushes forth like wind, like the heat in July on the plains. It is difficult to see. Ahmet and Nevart immediately seek out the other children to slide along the marble floor and play games with. The dome above their heads lets in little light; the hanging oil lamps contribute to the already heavily laden atmosphere. Gülhan Hanim and Anaguil go in search of an available sink along the wall of the huge chamber.

There are numerous white marble sinks dotting the round walls of the large circular room; the hamam embraces the women tightly like an opaline cup. Each sink has running hot water from the central heating fire that is kept burning day and night throughout the year. It is the fire which has burned in the bathhouse for over three hundred and twenty years. Gülhan Hanim approaches an unused sink and pulls the rag from the spout to let the water flow forth and then she washes her hands and feet and face. She places her feet back into the straps of her sandals and wipes her face with the small towel Anaguil gives her. Anaguil repeats the same ablutions and they go through the steam toward the centre of the chamber seeking the hot marble circle.

The steam flows around them and through the blue-glass dome above like sun rays coalesced with milk. The sweating begins, at the temples, on the arms, in the armpits, behind each knee, in the groin: the secretions of impurities flow and run and dribble to the stone floor – like juice, like sweet sugar-water, like pomegranate-seed milk, like menstrual blood. Gülhan Hanim and Anaguil lie on the marble floor, each to contemplate her own body's purging and thirsts. It is hot and the odours of body come in and out of Anaguil's mouth.

Anaguil holds her arms straight at her sides, her elbows and knuckles lock. Her head is turned away from Gülhan Hanim. She stares aimlessly through the impenetrable bath air. She enters the music deliberately; she is moving outside of the bathhouse in 1917, in April, outside of the round blue and condensed room where she recognizes no friends or family except for her 'auntie' Gülhan Hanim and little Nevart. The sweat streams from her. What goes with it? she wonders. Where could I travel if I were to follow the path of my own sweat and piss, down which alleyways and rain gutters would I wander? Would they lead me back to some place where I could recognize myself?

The heat is like weight and then the heat is like weightlessness. The baths and the women pull her in. There are now women everywhere, lining every inch of white marble floor, unblocking sinks; there are children, boy and girl children, sliding along the resting areas. There are whispered whisperings, talkings, conversations and small laughter. There is indecipherable noisiness. Sighs.

Emine Hanim's daughter, that girl over there.

The older woman lying to Anaguil's left gestures to her companion, pointing towards a young girl across the room.

Such an ugly bosom. One so much smaller than the other, like a plum and a melon. And bow legs, chhhst, bad luck – few children can be supported by them. I hoped she'd come today so that we could get a proper look at her. So much subterfuge these days from the young girls.

Did you see the mark on her back, Nigaz Hanim? Or notice her hirsute limbs? What man would desire that ugly mule? No, that girl's not for my boy. When he comes home from the front, I'll find him a real beauty.

When my Fevzi comes home, I'll cook him his favourite dish and tell him honestly. Fevzi, I'll say, these girls are not good enough for you.

And so skinny that one over there, you can see the rib bones. What man wants a bony mare? But look

27

there, that one over there. Do you see her? She's the daughter of Bedri Agha. She has narrow wrists and perfect proportions. Her skin is like the freshest cheese!

Yes, perhaps she is the one. I'll send Pars to the letter-writer this afternoon with my instructions. I'll tell him to pen a letter: Fevzi, my little-king, I'll say, your an-ne misses you. I have seen a goodgirl for you. She will make you happy and give you many sons. Fevzi, my dearest, go to the letter-writer soon. Your an-ne has had no news from you in months.

Anaguil concentrates on the pores of her skin opening wide, like so many cupping hands. They hold the heated room. Her eyelids drop and then two and more beads of perspiration slide from her temples, as if originating out of the air and her skin together, out of a chemical reaction, so that there are blue beads sliding down her cheeks. She tries to follow each drop, to distinguish each droplet of sweat as one would pick out a piece of hard candy from a bowl. There is no music now. She holds the beads in her mind and she breathes deeply into her lungs when she remembers to breathe deeply, and then slowly, with just that breath, the muscles in her back below and above her shoulder blades loosen like an unfolding ball of yarn; they begin to spread out across the bathhouse like an unfurled spring. I am hungry for oranges, she thinks. And brine cabbage pickles. Tourshi. She loses the glassy beads at her jaw, at the line drawn there by her bone: they scatter or evaporate. I would like the crisp watermelon from our garden.

Anaguil tightens her arm muscles and she grasps and rolls and tugs the unfolded yarn, the unfurled spring back into her taut back. She uncups her soft

28

hands and lays them out on the marble as if they too were made of limestone. She hates the hamam now. She hates the collusion of its seduction. Its ruthless indifference and reckless forgetting.

Eventually Gülhan Hanim lifts her head and says it's time to gather the children. They raise themselves from their places and go to find Ahmet and Nevart, who are giggling together with three other young Turkish children. One boy yells to Nevart as he sees the two women approaching.

Eh, Dilek, here come the Mommies.

Nevart quickly pulls her hands from her vagina where she had matter-of-factly been demonstrating what a girl's down-there looks like on the inside to the four children.

Anaguil hears nothing but the name: Dilek – *wish* in Turkish. Dilek. Dilek. And she sees how in very little time her four-year-old sister has become so, has become a Turkish-Mohammedan wish, and she knows not why the azure dome above her head will not crash down upon them all. Why the skies will remain standing. How it is that she can keep bursting open inside herself and not disappear or dissolve or become marbled dust. Perhaps it is the becoming of someone else. She herself is Fatma Hanim: a goodgirl.

They take the children into the next chamber and with the rough cloths they rub the bodies of the boy and girl; each child moans and complains and says that it is torture to their bodies. Anaguil says to Nevart in her ear: Quiet. This is no torture, little girl.

Chhht. See how dirty you are, little-king, Gülhan Hanim says.

Gülhan Hanim and Anaguil remove the wooden combs from the copper tray and begin to untangle the children's hair. Ahmet yells that it is like his skull is running through the teeth of the comb along with his hairs, but the combing is brief. For Nevart it is a lengthy process, to unbraid the scattered and tangled thick black hair and to begin at the ends which reach to her hips and slowly pull out the knots until the scalp is reached. Then there is more soap and more hot water. The children holler. The women shush them and when finished with the boy and girl, begin their own toilette.

Anaguil hands a loofah to Gülhan Hanim and takes one for herself from the tray. Anaguil rubs her arms, her legs, her belly and her breasts, the tops of her feet, and the backs of her thighs with an intense concentration. Her skin flushes and reddens and she likes the reddening, the change in colour and the good dullish sensation of rough and heat and open vulnerable skin to roughness; she likes the reminder of blood in the body; the small ways that small pains give her her thoughts.

The children wait impatiently for the women to finish; they are not allowed to leave the third room without them: it is dangerous for small children to walk alone on the slippery floors.

When Gülhan Hanim and Anaguil have finished scrubbing themselves, Anaguil removes the two oranges from the linen sack and begins to peel them. She gives half an orange to Ahmet and another to Nevart. She gives the second orange to Gülhan Hanim who is already eating tourshi. She herself takes nothing.

The bathhouse is confusing with the noise from the sinks and the lazy grinding of gossips. But it is also quieter now than it used to be; there is not as much ease now in the bodies or in the domed room. There is war in the waters, on the big ships, and on the damp skin. For some there is darkness as close as the dark pupil.

Gülhan Hanim, Anaguil, Ahmet and Nevart re-enter the main bathhouse – all the women in the central room have loosened their hair and it flows to the white marble floor and together it weaves a tapestry: a black-brown carpet. But there are gaps also, the hair is testimony to the missing strands. The two women and the children pass through to the outer chamber where the fountain first greeted them; they rush to the changing balcony and they dress quietly: the children are quiet also. The ugly Hamamjee-Khatoon is uglier still as Gülhan Hanim, Anaguil, Ahmet and Nevart leave the central bathhouse. They are clean; they have left very little behind.

They climb the mulberry tree together: Mama, the young scholar and Anaguil. It is spring and the air is thicker than usual with jasmine blossoms, white acacia blossoms, rose and lilac. They are high up in the tree and they begin to pick the mulberries, laughing all the while.

Mama says, Anaguil-eh, you look so pretty in this tree. Your cheeks are full and pink. Have you washed your hands and feet yet?

Mama takes out a paring knife from her pocket and finely slices each tiny mulberry in half. They are like golden red drops of dew.

Don't you wish you could save each one? she says.

Anaguil looks at Mama and is happy. She is happy also that the too-thin young man is in the tree with them, his head neatly affixed to his body. She thinks she will stay here for now, in this tree with Mama and the young scholar. She wonders where Jirair and Stepan and Nishan have run off to – are they watching little blue-eyed Nevart closely?

Mama says, Anaguil, my white dove, it's time to take the bread from the tonnir. Anaguil smiles, her stomach grumbling in anticipation of the fresh home-made bread they will eat with butter and mulberry jam. She drops to the ground in anticipation.

Then the girl Anaguil awakens. In her stomach there is a sensation like heavy and tarnished brass. Nevart is by her side sleeping soundly. The brief joy from the mulberry tree outside her old home in her old home's garden is an acridness in her mouth. There is today and the next day and the next, and there are chores to be done, she thinks. Anaguil turns over, pressing her body against her sister's; she wishes again for the world of sleep. She fears the world of dreams. But at least, perhaps, if one prays, and she does, Mama will come again. Mama will comfort her. Mama will smile.

Anaguil, my white dove, you hold my heart in your hands, Mama will say.

Rachel Eskijian, b. 1900, a Catholic Girl

The name of the place called forth the picture of the hills and the one flat road which ran through the middle of the town. Every other road in the town was steep and creviced; each alley was tight and dark like the interior of a thinly stretched and unpinkened sheep's skin for holding water. On these narrow streets where children, or later the Christians when invisible in manner, could walk unnoticed – I was born. In these hills, overlooking the plains of Anatolia that reached out for miles to Mount Ararat rising above in the west, I could almost see Noah's arcing hand as it waved back to us, the devout children miles away and below on the smaller hills of Kharphert, as I stood on the one flat road smiling but not waving my hand or expecting celestial trumpeting. In the plains below us lay the other town, Mezre, smaller and untangled at the base of the hills.

But I was three miles closer to God than the people of Mezre. In the hills and crags, close to the Euphrates College and to the American missionary-run elementary and secondary schools and to the French

Franciscan school for girls where I studied and prayed, close to the church where I worshipped, I lived, closer to God. This is where I died, also, close by, in the well not five hundred yards from the front gate of the school. It was eight months after the French sisters departed (they piled their crucifixes and blue rosary beads and French Catholic Holy Book onto the wagons along with their habits and sharp rulers and *Grammaires Françaises* just before war was declared in the fall of 1914); it was before Mother died or Arshanig or Vergeen, but after Missak and Vahan and Hovannes had been taken. (Will there be enough ink and parchment to transcribe the lists?) In a drinking well of closed eyes. There.

So that not the bayonets or the humping soldiers. So that not the piles of unshodden troops marching on the plains below and then eating in our classrooms and smoking in our private chambers after they'd moved up and made them their barracks. So that not the mark of sofkiat on our front door, quickly written in Arabic letters indicating the Turkish meaning in black charcoal. So that not that word *exile*. So that not the lice crawling through the town bedding and uncarded wool stores, rinsed first with kerosene and then with vinegar (to protect the scalp) and then combed out, the corpses on the floor like black dew. So that not the other words pleading in the queue outside the American dignitary's house – the Mr Davis house – our uncle our uncle our uncle who lives in Pennsylvania. So that not that No No No, Next. So that not when the butcher and the copper-shiner and the lazy-one-eye who fixed broken pottery and the veil-cloud of Mohammed's women descended like cherubim onto our streets, taking the copper pots, the rugs, kilims, the extra shoes, the mauve European dress, the bowls, clay pitchers, brass trays, silver urns, wall hangings and spoons, et cetera, et cetera, et cetera, out of our houses. Freely. So that not their laughing like sharp air in a tin box hitting the eight corners as if the box were a theatre and the theatre were a metal box between the eyes like an invisible shelf. So that not that, none of that, hastened me.

I looked over the plains of Anatolia, I remember, I wrote it down, and I could not smell the rotting things, and I could not see into the wild dog's mouth who carried the tibia of a relative, or of the boy two houses away who bothered me, back from the stinking plain and Lake Goeljuk. What became a matter was the view, the mountain of Noah, the sun and the lightening blue sky, all of the weather, and I laughed as I walked and I shook their tin between my brows like a tambourine on my hip, because there was no one in the blind alleyways. It was a moment in time between gendarmes walking, marking doors and pulling the What-are-you-doings? and the Not-me's! and the He-has-done-nothings! onto the packed dirt. The clubfoot Turkish boy crier yelled on each corner as he stumbled: Three thousand more killed! Our armies will be victorious! So I made my way to the French nuns' school, Our Lady of Sorrows, established in 1846 when the first French missionaries came to our end of the earth and mused, *Les chrétiens orientaux, ils peuvent-être sauver, n'est-ce pas?*

I cut my hair after I removed the black veil and I left my hair on the stone coping of the well. I spit my redmetal spittle after I had cut out my tongue because I refused to scream and thus I prevented screaming. Me, a Christian girl whom they nominated devil's cunt

35

and cuntwhore and infidel-bitch and wiping their boots on my hair swore I would be the bearer of a Mohammedan child into this world; and they filled the metal tin they had put there, made their music, and me, I would not – I refused. And as I flew into the well and through the air, the dark air which caressed my skin like warm-water silk, my thoughts were of the spring fields between plantings and their clusters of poppy flowers (red yellow orange white and pink) because of their unexpected brightness in my mind as the bricks moved in front of my eyes, wet and slick and dullblack, one after another, twelve, thirteen, fourteen, the bricks of the well near the school, not five hundred yards from my schoolyard. Bricks and thousands and thousands of red and yellow and orange and white and pink poppy flowers flew by me. And your words also, Father, came to me like a song as I flew into the well, you who said strength comes from the bone marrow when you will feel His Son and His Suffering Flesh. Can the blind lead the blind? Shall not both fall into the ditch? And I remembered Rachel's suffering and how she swore to Jacob that she would die without children and how she died on the birthing stool. And I thought how my name had impressed its regimen onto my skin, deep to the very bones.

When I died (and there is that moment like any other moment) after hitting the stones and after counting all of the bricks – one thousand three hundred and three – and after the water and the bodies of the Armenian girls who had beat me there (later there would be too many of us in the well for any other girl to join) and after picking my bouquet for you, Father, I went to heaven just like the Bonne Soeur Marie Marguerite had promised us we were destined to. The

Angel Gabriel swung the gates wide open to me and smiled and you, Father, and dear (hokees!) brothers ran out to greet me and I kissed your right hand, Father, as I kneeled at your feet and you touched my shoulder and I realized that I had saved all of us in my flight: there was no shame in heaven. And later when Mother and the younger sisters arrived from the Der-el-Zor, their skin a thick green like the flesh of an olive, a green no one expected from the monochrome of the Arabian landscape, I greeted them and we kissed and hugged and we resumed family life. (All of this with the wide-open eyes.) Which for me meant knitting stockings for each member of the family and perfecting the fine art of Armenian lace and embroidery, Italian filet and Swiss drawnwork on linen. I picked through piles of beans for small bits of rock and other debris. In the good weather of Paradise we took daily walks in the sun.

Death is a question of calibration. The deepest chambers of the Inferno are notched like wooden sticks, not by increasing heat and fire as Dante thought (and the Soeurs de Charité instructed us) but by the increasingly unadulterated steps of memory, steppes of memory which extend into infinity like the plains of Anatolia had extended before us, brick upon brick like the deep insides of a well. In the deepest reaches of Hell there is so much knowledge that all of eternity stretches out in time, day after day, the knowing like a separation; a timeless loneliness for every soul, for all of the days in Hell.

In Paradise there is no past, only blissful present, and Eve walks naked among us and she too has forgotten those below still living in Kharphert and further below in Mezre.

And I have all of my family with me in heaven, and most of my girlhood friends. I can speak, but I no longer need to.

I wrote down what I cannot, in my glory, remember any more: it is a story. I stuffed the words into a crevice at the top part of the well where the Cavass of Consul Davis of America would later hide the photographs of Lake Goeljuk. They were the pictures that Mr Davis could not take with him when the Americans joined the Great War and he fled on horseback with his portmanteau and his modern ink pens and his gold pocket watch.

It is written there that heaven and earth shall pass away: but my words shall not pass away (Luke 21:33).

I copied this also.

Mamouret-ul-Aziz (Harput), Turkey
June 2, 1914

My Dear Catharine,

I arrived two days ago to the Harput Consulate, safe and sound in health despite the delays and obduracy of my Turk guides. I had intended to mail some letters along the way, but on the road we only passed through farming villages where I was told a posted letter had little chance if any of reaching its destination. Thus I determined to wait until my arrival here to send you news of the assignment and the journey from Batum.

For the length of the overland journey from Samsun on the Black Sea to the region of Harput, I was obliged to ride in a wagon (for appearance's sake I did not press the issue of riding horseback with the guards), so that by the time we arrived to the Consulate, almost two weeks later, I was of a sore temper indeed. The landscape of Asiatic Turkey is often desolate, and the road traversing the mountains is steep and narrow and sometimes treacherous. The wagons often moved at a terribly slow pace. At times I was sure I could have walked more briskly than our transport! I wished again and again that I could have ridden by horseback.

Upon our arrival to the district, I received a surprise when my Turk companions indicated that I would be staying in the town of Mamouret-ul-Aziz, called Mezre by the local inhabitants. They assured me that the consular building is actually located there, three miles distant from Harput, my official documents notwithstanding. The town of Mamouret-ul-Aziz, where one finds the seat of local government, and our new residence, is located at the base of a small mountain, atop of which one finds Harput. Mamouret-ul-Aziz is currently only about half the size of Harput, about 15,000 inhabitants, but is growing rapidly.

I have been pleased to discover that the consular building is one of the finest in the country, most likely in the whole interior of Asia Minor. As it turns out, Consul Peters was a terrible bookkeeper and a dismal registrar, but apparently quite a patron of things Oriental – you will be amazed (as was I) at the fine collection of rugs, pictures and furniture which he amassed. The building is large and constructed of limestone, it stands three stories high and in the back is surrounded by an immense garden filled with many types of trees including mulberry, apricot and pine. There are very high walls surrounding the gardens, so we shall have our privacy here. In short, there shall be no Mr Gottshalk peering over my shoulder with disdain for my 'rough country bearing' and 'uncouth manners'. Although he may have believed this assignment was some kind of embarrassment for me, I am determined he shall be proven wrong.

Currently the Orientals' most important industry is agriculture, but it is believed that the railroad begun in Samsun will reach Harput within two years, thereby increasing communication and commerce with the outside world. Business here will then flourish and the commercial work for a consul will consequently increase. As this region develops, my posting here will be considered more highly. I look forward to seeing Mr Gottshalk then! Harput is already the most important mission station for the American Board of Commissioners for Foreign Missions, perchance it will become a thriving place of trade. I think we can be happy here, Catharine.

I am told there is a beautiful lake not ten miles from the town called Goeljuk. Next summer we will camp on its banks for the hottest months just as my predecessors have always done. We can sleep underneath the stars, or as you prefer in a large canvas tent. We shall have everything we need, including cooks and water-carriers. As I become settled I find that life in the Orient, however unrefined, can be rather pleasant. The local peoples are Mohammedan Turks and Kurds and Christian Armenians, and although they physically resemble one another, their customs, habit of dress and religious practices vary considerably. For the most part, they are a friendly and hospitable people. I am affronted by some of their habits, particularly as regards questions of hygiene, but that is to be expected. Our situation in the Consulate, however, is really quite fine and civilized.

You shall meet some of the young missionary ladies when you arrive. There are the Misses Campbell and Jacobsen of Amherst, and the wife of Dr Atkinson of Boston, whom I have met and who look forward to your arrival in the near future. In all, there are seventy-five foreign missionaries in this region, or 'vilayet' as they say here. I am told Miss Campbell is as fond of Keats as you are!

I have begun to investigate a southern route to Harput, one that traverses the Mesopotamian plain, and in this way avoids the steep mountainous passes of the north. We can meet in Beyrouth and travel by train to Ras-ul-Ain and then by wagon via Urfa and Diyarbakir to Harput. I think this route will be easier and more pleasant than the one I have just traveled, so do not worry about the strain of the journey. I am pleased to hear you are faring much better, and that you are over your disappointment at having to depart Batum last year and return to New York to recuperate. I will send news soon of exactly how and when we may meet in Beyrouth.

Do not neglect to pack your sturdy shoes for the Orient, Catharine, for the roads are primitive. Give my love to Katy and pack a pound of Dillard Chocolates for me. I do miss confections from home!

41

It's been too long, my dear – this last year of separation has been difficult.

I am, as always,

Your admiring and loving husband,
Leslie

TELEGRAM SENT

DEPARTMENT OF STATE

HARPUT. TURKEY.   JUNE 10, 1914

CATHARINE DAVIS.

RECEIVED YOUR TELEGRAM INFORMING ME OF
FATHER'S ILLNESS. HAVE BEEN GRANTED
LEAVE OF ABSENCE. WILL ENDEAVOR TO BE
HOME BY END OF JULY. LESLIE DAVIS.

Alexandria, Egypt
August 23, 1914

My Dear Catharine,

I send you this quick note via an American businessman, Mr Thomas Nesbit, who has agreed to post it upon his arrival in America (overland mail from the Orient is unpredictable now and slower than ever, as you may imagine, due to the turn of events).

I have just received instructions from the Department of State that I am to return to my post in Harput. I know I should not consider personal feelings but my disappointment is great. I fear that I will not see Father again and I am saddened to hear of his suffering. I can only hope that this war will be over in a matter of months as many here are surmising and that I in some small way may be of service.

Alexandria is a beautiful city, one I'd dreamed of visiting and one I'd hoped to share with you. Now I must turn back immediately. Who can say what the next months will bring? Keep me in your thoughts and prayers as I keep you in mine.

I remain,

Your loving husband,

Leslie

Did It Make You Ache So, Leaving Me?

Tonight I am thinking. In the space of evening calm, as I look through my small glass window up at the stars in the night sky, I am wondering what it is that provokes men's actions. How it is that there is something more terrible in men than in any beast. And I've been pondering the nature, the very thing, that is terrible. Shall I call it Evil? Does it live in all of us, regardless of blood or kin, like a viper waiting in the hollow of a fir tree? Should we step lightly around the perimeter of every fir tree? Do we all carry hollows, and in them this *thing*, expectant?

When I was a boy I saw a snake, like a coiled whip, in the garden. I spied the beast at the moment I perched to step into its circle; his head was high and lifted towards me, daring me to tread. I jumped that day, and ran screaming, Hayrig! The Devil's in the garden! He's come for me.

I ran into the house, thinking that the snake was coming in directly after me, set to lunge for my throat. But when I glanced behind me, I was alone and the garden was quiet and I could hear the tumbling water of the fountain and the scratching of grapevines against the bower. I heard the grapes explode and their sugar-sweet juice splash the dirt, delighting the red ants that lived there.

For years after that, I always carried an air rifle with me into the garden and I tried to kill every snake that I could find a target for. Hayrig used to laugh at my antics, my prowling through the bushes. They're harmless, son. Why kill what brings no pain?

Yet he never stopped me and I was a very good shot.

Now I think about that snake of my childhood and my childhood nightmares and I think: they were figments of an overactive mind, they were not deadly and fierce. This, now, this keeping of a man dressed in a woman's clothes in the attic of his home and reading by a small candle so as not to call attention from the street, and still covering the small window with black cloth, this is something deadly and fierce and coiled and ready to strike. And that is not the deadliest. It is the waiting.

(I cannot help but wonder, did we do some *thing* to bring this down upon our heads?)

Today when Mairig went to the marketplace with some neighbour women because there were no men to go to market, and nine- and ten-year-old Turkish boys spat on them, on my mama and the neighbour women, was there something in particular that made those boys hateful? Had they been listening to their fathers complain and sermonize on the 'Filthy Infidel'? Had they heard the town crier announce the *coup d'état* that the Armenians were planning? Did they *believe* we were going to revolt? Or were they simply shocked by women in the marketplace? Only able to associate whores with the handling of money in public?

45

Had those nine- and ten-year-old boys believed wholeheartedly in their ideas? Their ideas like a coiled garden serpent?

Perhaps nothing. Perhaps Evil is an ancient and colossal bird of prey that roams the countryside and swoops down into towns and villages unexpectedly, dropping its little turds of blackness into otherwise unpolluted human hearts. Perhaps it loves a good shit.

It is not as if I am only now learning to hate them. We have always feared their capacity. There have been too many reasons and mass killings over these many years. It is not as if I don't fear them in every way – only to think of them at night as I sit awake and wait for dawn, smoking all the tobacco Mama has given me, gives me the instant urge to defecate. Food no longer remains inside the body, it rushes from me like a hurried traveller anxious to arrive at his destination. This fear gives me no rest from licentious thoughts and urges. (What I wouldn't give for my thoughts to materialize.) An arse, a pulled thigh.

My books see me with their pages laid open wide to the world and to my growing cock: they are witness to my bodily functions, they do not judge me for them. Sometimes I give a little bit of my seed to these books, like a farmer will fertilize his crop. As in the years before God, when the ancients honoured the spirits of the fields and streams and moon.

Yet I think: you won't grow. My books and I will have the same fate.

Will I die at the hands of Mustafa the reed-sharpener, who delicately shaped the points of the reeds I bought from him as a young boy once or twice a month? Or Sinan the bath-attendant, who always frowned as we entered through the thick wooden doors with Father, and then winked slyly when we turned to have a look? Would it be better if my killer were someone I have known in my life? Someone I bought wheat from in the market, or butter, on a weekly basis? Or my favourite sweet? Sweetmeat? Mairig's silver tea service?

Did it make you ache so, leaving me?

Hakan would say, Eench-spesez, Sargis? in Armenian, and I would answer him back, tapping down my smile each time, La-vem. Hakan with the big black eyes, and dark brown hair like a cape which always flew into them. He was one of a handful of Turkish students at the college. His father, Aziz Bey, was a forward-thinking man who insisted that his son learn English fluently. Despite Aziz Bey's money and position, Hakan was always an outsider; the atmosphere in the college touched him with a cold hand. The young men had few words for the Turkish philologist.

In the spring of 1913 I went to watch the football match between two groups of students. I sidled up to the field with my book in my hand and I sat in the grasses watching the gracefulness of the men moving up and down the playing field; their muscles flexed in the afternoon sun beneath their trousers and long shirts, like waves beneath a tarp. A few yards away I saw the Turkish boy with a book in his hand also, his lithe body stretched out on the grass. I couldn't make out the book title but I was curious so I stood and I approached him, and he looked up at me and shaded his eyes with his hands, and his hair like a cape flew up into his eyes, only to be stopped by the shielding hand. His red fez lay discarded near the crook of his elbow.

Hello. Do you read something interesting today? I

47

asked, in stiff English. And he, still looking at me, lifted his fez and placed it on his head. The black tassel fell onto his cheek. He lifted his hand and flipped it back and smiled with his beautiful mouth showing his square teeth and shining gums. He stood up.

Iyo, he said in Armenian, as if he'd been waiting, prepared for the day when one of us would approach him: Whit-man.

I smiled at him. How do your studies progress?

I gestured that we sit and then I bent down to the hot dry grass; the sun was in my eyes now. The upper classmen from the college continued their sweating and swearing as they ran up and down the field.

Quite well, thank you.

We sat together until the end of the match, he and I, Hakan and I, the objects of no great interest or particular distaste.

I didn't know that day (if I had known, would I have remained seated in my own patch of sun and watched silently and alone the movement of the waves, the ocean of bodies gathering and thundering up the field crying foul! every so often?) that he would teach me to love someone who is not supposed to be loved. I didn't know that you, Hakan, boy of the dipping hair and the eyes like questions, would be my tutor. I was the boy who made my father proud: the scholar, the professor a few years hence, the one who would go to Constantinople and perhaps to France or England and America.

And I had always admired Koharig, the neighbour's girl. Her smell, her light brown hair, pulsing wheat in the summer. Her gambol smile. They were as familiar to me as my dreams, and I dreamed until I soiled myself. But, I dreamed of you also. Your back and

48

pulled thighs, your teeth and your beautiful mouth. Now, as I wait to see who will be my executioner (Will it be you? Or have you joined the army in the Dardanelles? Are you starving on the Russian steppes?) I have no shame left. I am a man who shits in his pants like a babe. You made me love someone who is not supposed to be loved. If you could see me now, would you save me, anoushig Hakan? Or would you pop out my eyes and send the white and brown and red spheres to Mairig for tea as your father did with the neighbour woman's son?

We didn't know then that that life would change irrevocably in the fall of 1914. In April of that year I taught you, Your mother is a donkey! and we laughed when you swore beneath your breath in Armenian at the young men in our class who dared not even look at you.

You confided in me that you dreamed of being a scholar, that you wanted to spend your life reading books and writing treatises, but Aziz Bey had other plans for you. You would be a public servant. First an officer in the army. Perhaps one day vali of our vilayet.

You lived in Mezre and some days you refused the horse your father provided, and you walked up the hill to Kharphert and to the college. We found abandoned places together in town – a small fountain behind a mosque, a shut-up doorway, a huddle of trees, my father's garden in the middle of the day when he was away on business and mother and the servants were busy with their chores – and we introduced each other to poetry.

And in my soul I swear I will never deny him.

The world opened up to us. It seemed possible then to defy our fathers and become Poets. I would be the next Sayat'-Nova and Hakan yearned to be a forbidden poet – you said you would be forbidden; you introduced me to the American Whitman. Your private tutor slipped his book into your hands the year before and you were transformed.

You whispered,

The efflux of the soul comes from within through
   embower'd gates,
ever provoking questions,
These yearnings why are they? These thoughts in the
   darkness why are they?

And I understood you completely, my friend. I plucked a still-green apricot from the tree and I offered it to you.

I read to you in Armenian:

I come from very far and bring
with me dizzy riches,
I load the casket with priceless rubies.

You heard the cadence and dip of my language. There was no need to translate.

I haven't seen you since fall of last year, Hakan. I hope your uniform fits you well. I am sure you have boots, unlike so many of the soldiers who come through Kharphert. Yes, I have been moved to pity by the sight of the Turkish Kurdish bands, these ragged bone men who march along silently and leave their blood in cups.

I hope you are eating.

Do you stand on the prow of a ship in the straits?

50

Can you see Europe from where you stand? Can you still taste freedom in your mouth as you string English words together in your mind? The words of the American poet placed carefully on your lips.

> *This hour I tell things in confidence,*
> *I might not tell everybody, but I will tell you.*

The foreign tongue made everything seem possible, no?

Inside, 1917

She touches her collarbone, then its hollow, her skin is dry and smooth; she runs her second and index fingers into the groove of the hollowed collarboned space. Anaguil thinks of her birth and its obligations. She thinks of death not as if she wants to die, but as if her death were a trapped moth pressing upon her lower back side with its wings, in the space of her back where her kidneys ache – the space inside where the moth flies and flutters ensnared by the skin. Constant. Constantly. She digs her fingers into her skin.

She feels transfixed by the swirls and turns on the pads of her fingers, with the pink embedded or red embedded into the beige cushions. She has looked at her hands and in sixteen years she has not seen them; they are the familiar that becomes invisible: maelstrom skin. The Der Hyre said, To heaven when you die, but she wonders as she stares and bites and licks her fingertips: what of this? These lines across my wrist like interlacing chokers, like tangled gold. These grooves. Eddies. These palm-rivers: how can they cook, shape letters, scratch scabs raw again, comb the hair and touch where they want or perhaps they should not, those places that comfort and warm the hands? What happens to these things?

She touches herself to remember. Mama. Mama: I don't know if I can remember you in this skin and bone, collarbone, you gave me on the day of my birth. Enough.

She is writing a book of memory on her body and destroying it as she writes.

Baba – to see you again I would cut off my hand.
I could laugh like our chatty nightingale.

File No. 820.3, Page 3

❧❧❧

A remarkable thing about the bodies that we saw was that nearly all of them were naked. I have been informed that the people were forced to take off their clothes before they were killed, as the Mohammedans consider the clothes taken from a dead body to be defiled. Another remarkable thing was that nearly all the women lay flat on their backs and showed signs of barbarous mutilation by the bayonets of the gendarmes, these wounds having been inflicted in many cases probably after the women were dead.

Davis looks up from his papers as Lucine walks into the room bearing a tray of tea and afternoon gateaux. He places his fountain pen on the report he has been filing and watches her closely as she approaches him with his requested hot drink; she has covered her hair today with a black headscarf. Lucine reaches the immense desk and carefully places the copper tray on the intricate black and white inlay.

Mr Davis sir, your beverage. She lifts the gold and red painted saucer with the small glass cup of black tea towards him. Davis receives it across the expanse of wood. His fingers brush along hers.

Lucy, he says, as Lucine drops her hand to the tray and lifts the plate of cakes and places it on the desk within his hands' reach.

How are your English lessons progressing? Are the children learning quickly? He sips his tea.

Yes, quickly, sir.

He reaches for a date cookie and pops it in his mouth.

It's difficult to work without primers. Are you managing?

Yes, sir.

She stares at the small rosettes and floral figures dancing around the border of the woollen carpet beneath the desk.

The children must be kept occupied. Do you wear the naphthaline bands I gave you?

No, sir. They hurt the skin.

Ah, Lucy. You know you must protect yourself.

He rises from his chair and comes around the side of the desk to stand beside her. Lucine picks up the copper tray and turns to face the door of the salon, staring now at the large hexagonal figure woven into the centre of the woollen rug: red geometry on a field of white.

Davis places his hand on the nape of her neck.

You're a goodgirl . . .

Lucine counts the rosettes on the white field of knotted wool.

I'm melancholy today. A man has his melancholy moments.

Lucine is reminded of Miss Robertson, the first American lady she knew at the missionary-run elementary school where she studied as a girl. She recalls the young miss saying, Good morning, girls, today is a glorious day for God's work. The class repeating dutifully and in unison: Good morning, Miss Robertson, yes indeed!

She never understood this word *indeed* and she does not know his word: *melancholy*. She waits and Davis laughs.

With a bit of exercise I'll feel better. Tell Mrs Kazanjian if we can have anything other than pilaf for supper I'd be much obliged.

He runs his hand down Lucine's back slowly as he speaks, clipping her vertebrae. He rests his index finger in the indent of her lower back for the briefest moment, there in that body dip. Lucine can hear his breathing as she stares, silent, at the floor. He lifts his hand. She waits, sensing but not seeing his movements: she feels him raise his hand to his nose and breathe deeply. Davis walks back behind the monstrous desk.

Thank you, Lucy.

She understands her cue, and turns and walks towards the door.

Dickran, Whose Name Went Unrecorded

 infinitesimal

I was born in 1915 on the Anatolian plateau, beneath a ubiquitous sky whose iridescent blue was like a fine lace veil covering my eyes. I saw the world through the openings and around the edges of the scalloped filet. I remember seeing the reaching branches and green leaves of the oak tree like hands in prayer, the grooves in the brown-grey tree bark like empty rivers, and the drifting of woolly cloud shapes like prehistoric beasts. I didn't know what to call these blue-edged pictures before my eyes, but I saw them clearly in the hours before my death.

This I know: I was born Dickran, second child and first son to Mariam and Hovsep, the son of Boghos, in the Armenian village of Bozmashen. I was conceived six months before my father's conscription into the armed forces, when he left our home at night with his wrists bound behind his back, secured by a tether to his brother, my Amo Vahram. In the light of the kerosene lamp, my father noticed that the ropes the gendarmes used to tie them with were already stained with blood. He asked the gendarmes politely as they pulled his arms high behind his back: Effendi, is it necessary to tie the arms of men who will serve in the Great Ottoman Army and defend the Empire? Shut your mouth! they said, as if they had answered the question before, and then pushed my father and uncle through the front door and into the night. We did not hear from or see them again (actually, I never saw them at all). But like all the families in our village we heard the rumours about the lake, and in the weeks after all of the men between the ages of sixteen and forty-five had been conscripted, we thought the feral dogs looked fatter. The birds of prey stayed out on the plains and let the mice in the village run freely.

I was conceived months earlier, in December, when the snow had piled up past the mud-brick walls to our tiled rooftops. It was the season when the neighbours did their visiting by walking from roof to roof and coming in through a trap door in the ceiling. Eyaa, brothers! the visitor would exclaim, and my father would open the hatch in the ceiling to admit him.

The men would then sit on the cushions and smoke from the water pipe while my mother, my little-mama, our mairig, heated the water with coffee and sugar and served it in delicate demitasses.

There is no news about the Dardanelles, Gaspar reported that winter morning. The fighting continues. Garo Hoogasian says he has heard that the soldiers have no shoes.

Basturmaji-Gaspar, meat-curer-Gaspar as he was affectionately called, then lifted his head and exhaled a blue smoke. Have you any suggestions, Digin Hampartzoum, he asked my nene, for a very bad chest cold? Arpine is sick again.

A bit of hollyhock flower boiled into a tea, my nene

responded, and rose from her seated position to go to the storeroom. When she returned she offered our visitor a small bundle of dried flowers and her best wishes for his wife.

Tell her five cups a day, Nene said, to be sipped slowly.

On this day of my conception, the family stayed indoors all day because of the terrible cold outside. By five o'clock, Mairig had already unearthed a head of cabbage from the storeroom floor and made dolma which she served with pilaf. My old nene yelled out after she had tasted her portion: As usual, this requires more salt, Daughter-by-marriage. Mairig said nothing, as is our custom.

After the meal, the men began their card games; Mairig continued the weaving of that winter's kilim, and my nene spun wool at the spinning wheel. Everyone was gathered in a circle around the tonnir, some with their feet tucked tightly under the red and black and cream woollen blankets to keep warm. My sister, Arsinee, dozed lightly next to Mairig. Soon Nene began to tell stories of the djinn and then of the heroic feats of Dickran-the-Great-King-of-Kings, and Mairig brought out the dried golden raisins and spread them atop the blanket.

Eat, hokees, Nene said to Arsinee. You can still taste summer in these fruits.

At nine o'clock the family retired to their sleeping pallets. Mairig slept facing the wall in the far corner of our two-room house (in the other room the sheep, goats and chickens slept). Just as Mairig was falling into sleep, picturing the house where she had been raised, and just as she was beginning to run towards the cool brook with her girlhood friends, my father began lifting her shift from behind. He lifted it quietly. And then, over the light snoring of Nene across the room, he did what was accepted and expected and Mairig did the same. As Mairig stared at the wall before her, which she could barely make out in the late-night darkness of the house, she felt a bead of sweat from her husband's brow fall onto her exposed nape.

I came to my brief consciousness with the rhythm of walking – it awakened me. Mairig walked for weeks and I could feel the rhythm of our days like a constant pull of tides, although I never knew the tides; the walking was boundless and finally it pulled me from Mairig's womb. I turned and I was pressed into the noise and light and streams of cold air at dawn in the open plains. And I discovered skin, mouth, teat, and the blue veil of this earth, and eventually urine and bowels.

The sky lay lightly and heavily upon all of us; it altered its shades with the course of the sun as we walked towards the Der-el-Zor: I saw blue like an iris from light to dark. After my delivery, my mother strapped me to her breast with a long swath of undyed wool turned dark brown from the constant dust of the caravans, and she continued walking. She walked with the other women and children and old men of our village. Bozmashen and twenty other Armenian villages were included in that particular caravan. We had been temporarily deported from our homes and relocated into the Der-el-Zor desert. We would return, assured the Turkish town crier, who had gone from village to village in the month of June announcing our departure dates. Take only what you will need, he yelled on each street corner, the rest you can leave in your dwellings until your homecoming. We are doing this for your safety, he affirmed.

Most residents of Bozmashen had never in their lives travelled more than twenty miles beyond the perimeter of the village. As the women packed the bundles and filled the knapsacks, as they prepared the families to leave the places where the clans had formed – during the time when history was still coupled in verse and was a troubadour's bread and butter – they comforted one another with small hopes. Perhaps we will find our men in Arabia, they said.

When the wagons were loaded and the bundles secured, the small children jumped up and down with delight, thinking that this thing called 'exile' would be a great adventure.

Later, on the open plains, the road stretched out in front of us with the walking herds of villagers – the hundreds of Anatolian Armenian clans – and it stretched behind us in ribbons of littered and broken bodies, mostly the old, the infirm and the very young. As the days passed the piles behind us seemed larger than the dusty figures in front of us. Our nene stayed back in one of those body-mounds. The abandoned voices followed us as we climbed up and down the mountains, skirting the local towns and the sources of running water at the gendarmes' insistence.

Ma-Ma, the voices said, do you have a cup of water and some bread?

With each subsequent day Mairig found it harder and harder to hold herself upright. And when her milk finally dried up, it is true that I cried for days. Sometimes Mairig passed me to Arsinee, who held me close and cuddled me for a little while.

Baby Dickran, you will be strong like Hayrig, she'd

61

say. And we will play together under the night sky. We will count the stars together. And we'll never again eat grass for our dinner.

In the third week after my birth, a group of Kurdish villagers descended upon us and stole the last of our possessions so that there was no cloth left to swaddle me, and I, like Mairig and Arsinee, was naked beneath the sun. Soon all of our skin changed from pink to darkest brown and then finally to the olive green that came off in sheaves.

Keep moving! our guards yelled. The constant sound of their whips slapping the hot air and bodies was like the sound of unbaked bread when it smacks against the cooking stone.

In the open plains there are few trees. When Mairig finally stumbled upon one, she stopped and she kissed me on my neck. And there underneath the oak tree I lay quietly, like a good boy, where my mairig left me. I did not scream and carry on like the other babies and young children lying next to me. My thirst for life was quieted by the majestic oak and the cloud shapes I could make out through the veil of blue lace which covered me.

A Turkish soldier saw the rows of babies settled around the tree and thought of his wife, who wanted another child. He miraculously took pity upon me and picked me up and carried me to his village and named me Ali. I became a good Muslim boy and I honoured my father and I recited passages from the Qur'ān better than any boy in the village. I grew to be quite tall and I loved the taste of dried raisins on my tongue. At night I was sometimes disturbed by dreams of a green-black face covered in tears. In the morning I said my prayers fervently.

62

No, it was not like that. It was a Kurdish woman whose own son had died from the infections that the miles of dead bodies brought to her village. And she took pity on the little Armenian boy Dickran, whose name she never would have known. And she wrapped me in colourful wool swaddling clothes and bounced me on her knobby knees. And although I never learned to read or write, I became an expert tanner and I made beautiful skins for twenty villages. When my wife bore our first son, I was the proudest man in the vilayet.

But if I tell you another story, you will understand: there were too many of us to safeguard beneath the few and bedraggled trees. The trees in the plains were full of babies and old fathers and old ladies whose mothers and daughters and nieces and wives and four-year-old sons had left them there. We stretched for miles across the deserted plains. If aeroplanes had flown above us they would have marvelled at the human sculpture we made with our thousands of bones and bodies becoming bones, with our skin and the fat underneath, which melted in the midday sun like soft clay. The vultures swooping in among us, and the wolves feeding themselves and their sucklings from us added their hungry delight to the tableau.

There were no thoughts in my mind, no language then to think it out, and no paper or fountain pen to write it down. The holy books and the holy houses had been burned. So I looked at the stars and I reached for them through the night blue coverlet with my small hands until I could touch the stars and then the heavenly bodies. That was how I was miracled into heaven.

The Smallest Animals

It is Friday and so they'll eat stuffed cabbage. Anaguil stuffs and rolls each softened leaf into a cylinder and places it into the copper pot while she hums. The words to a lovesong go round in her mind in a circular fashion: the song shape is like the shape of the dolma she is making: Sweet love, come, come take my soul, come and I will be shoes for your feet.

There's nothing happening now, Mama. The street looks like it's sleeping.

Stepan stands in front of the window clutching the curtain. Nishan and Jirair have become tired of the weeks of endless looking and so they sit in the corner playing backgammon. The dice click against the inlaid wooden board as the boys silently play.

Then come away, eh? We'll eat soon. Looking stops nothing. And it is quiet today. Yughaper flips her hand towards the window and her son and then back to her own body where it falls down slowly and lies like a child's sleeping form in her lap.

Daughter, the children should eat. Wake Nevart when the meal is ready.

Anaguil lifts her head from her concentration and her humming, and the wrapping, folding and placing of dolma into the large pot on the cooking stove. She looks at her mother whose age has become heavy in the past few months, whose thirty-four years have crept in suddenly, like corner-spiders. She begins to look like an old woman, Anaguil thinks, a spider in every crease and niche and crook.

Mama, are you hungry?

No, not now, Yughaper replies from the chair in which she sits facing the tonnir. This, she continues, tucking her chin towards the memory of warmth, makes me wish for the piled-up snow on the ground stepping past our doors and windows and up to our rooftops. Then who could look into or out of the glass? In winter it would be more difficult to round up the herds and send them to the fields and to the lake.

Ma-ma.

Anaguil stops the work of her hands. She rises from her kneeling position and pushes towards her mother. As she does, the half-filled pot edges off the cooking stove. The pile of stuffed cabbage dolma teeters precariously for a few moments inside the dull copper pot and then the pot drops with its heavy weight to the floor beneath – and spreads out the light green leaves, the loose cinnamon rice, the pinenuts currants filling. All of this happens suddenly, like a spray of coloured marbles that boys will play with in the springtime in the streets when there are boys out of doors. Stepan shoots a glare from the window.

See what's done to dinner!

Anaguil pulls her mother's hands out of her lap and presses one and then the other to her cheeks.

Mama, eench-eh? Eench-eh? She stares at the

flowers on her mother's dress, waiting for an answer.

Yughaper is so hot that she is cold and then hot again and then longing for the cold and for winter and for the snowy plains' pictures of Kharphert to whiten her mind, anything to take the open-field pictures from her eyes. Yughaper's gold wedding band, thick like a metal rope, slips from the base of her finger to its tip when she moves her hands from Anaguil's cheeks and places them back into her lap. The band does not register the changes in the woman since springtime; it no longer moulds to the hands that have become like wires. Anaguil looks at the yellow roses of her mother's dress and at her mother's clenched and changed hands.

Uf. I'm only a little tired. Clean up that mess and feed the boys.

Anaguil looks over her shoulder and sees the food strewn on the floor. She turns back to her mother.

Mama, I'll help you to bed. Yes? You must only sleep and you will feel better.

First pick up the dolma and clean it and put it back on the cooking stove. The boys must eat. Make sure, daughter. You are woman enough at fourteen to see that these children are properly cared for.

Yughaper then closes her eyes and appears to drift into sleep. Anaguil stands up and walks back towards the cooking stove and begins to pick up the bits of cabbage and nuts and rice. She picks up every scrap and piece. She wipes off any dirt she can see and she refolds the opened dolma and begins once again to build a pile inside the pot. No song comes to her mind. There is now a heaviness in her chest and to lift this heaviness she concentrates on the folding and rolling and placing of each cylinder into the heavy copper pot.

Stepan continues looking out into the early June evening. It's quiet now, is that better? he asks. Anaguil, what about our dinner?

The dice in the far corner of the room continue their clicking and spilling onto wood. Jirair and Nishan continue their gaming.

Once the fire has been lighted and the pot of dolma set to simmer, Anaguil returns to her mother's side. She gently lifts her mother up, grasping first the wire hands and then cupping her mother from behind like a soft push.

To bed, Mama. You must only sleep and you will feel better.

Anaguil guides Yughaper to her bedroom; Yughaper does not open her eyes. She lets her daughter remove her woollen shawl and summer shoes. Anaguil pulls the blankets back with one hand and then eases her mother down onto the bedding. Anaguil tucks the blankets around her mother's shoulders, leaving only her face exposed in the summer evening in the darkened house where the curtains are pulled tightly.

Mama, sleep well.

Yughaper noticeably trembles; her body moves in a slow shiver. She says nothing and Anaguil goes to check on the dinner and to make tea.

There are no limits, anoushig Anaguil.

Anaguil gets up from where she has been sitting next to her mother on the bed and douses the lamp.

In the dark Yughaper says slowly, Without them the dome of heaven collapses.

In the night Yughaper screams, and this from a woman who was always quiet, who, after her husband was taken in May, did not pull out her hair but spun wool unceasingly and then knitted a shawl and tucked it around her shoulders. On this night, on 18 June, one week before the clubfoot Turkish boy crier will stop on every corner in the Armenian quarter beating his drum, yelling, The decree from Constantinople demands that all Armenians be exiled to Arabia, Yughaper wakes the house with her screams.

There are bones in Arhana Maden. I see them, I see your Baba there. There are bones at Lake Goeljuk.

Anaguil runs to her mother's side.

Mama, wake up. It's dreaming, you're only dreaming.

Yughaper turns her open glass-brown eyes to her daughter.

No daughter, this is no dream.

She closes her eyes again and sleeps.

In the morning Anaguil goes to the American hospital. She describes her mother's symptoms to the nurses.

Miss Campbell says that it is lice. A louse could accomplish what a bayonet or wooden club took some effort to achieve. Perhaps not more than one bite, and against one bite what could be done exactly? Kerosene? Cold compresses?

Anaguil spies Dr Atkinson running from patient to patient; the Turkish soldiers are the only patients allowed in the hospital ward. He wears his naphthaline bands at his wrists and ankles.

Typhus, says the young American missionary. Lice bring the typhus disease.

The smallest animals are also defeating us, Anaguil thinks.

68

Spare the Rod

Maritsa, do you think you're a boy? An-ne scolded, rapping my hand with her switch.

I was three or four years old, not tall enough yet to reach the window. She didn't feed me that night or the next day.

I learned from such teachings not to stretch my hand out towards food, not to jump up and down, not to reveal joy in my facial expressions.

No one could have guessed then that I'd become beautiful.

Spotted mongrel, bow-legged bird, she called me.

The only times we regularly left the house and went out in public was to go to the hamam. As we walked to the bathhouse, I would drink in the world, trying not to let my an-ne or aunties see my pleasure, afraid they would take this small happiness from me. I glided through the streets imagining I was a princess, left behind somehow in the wrong house, in the wrong quarter, with the poorest of the poor: eleven of us women and four boys in the family.

There was only one window in our home and we

fought daily about who could stand in the best spot: Ayshegul, Fulya, Dilayur, Janan and I. The older women did not care so much – they were used to this life. It was the young girls who bickered constantly, circling around each other fitfully, like flies. The boys played in the corners or on the street; they occasionally became involved in our fights only to amuse themselves. They knew Uncle or Father would take them to market and to the coffee-house eventually, and perhaps to school if they were very lucky.

I have always been an indomitable girl – a girl with ideas. I beat the other girls away, fiercely I clung to the kafe – they left wailing and bruised and frightened; I swore I'd tear their eyes out. I stared out through the carved wooden squares and half-circles of the latticed shutter into the light of the street. I made up stories about the men and boys who passed beneath me. Sometimes their eyes would look up to the latticed window and I imagined they could see me, and that they would realize sooner or later their long-lost twin was awaiting them patiently – locked inside.

I spent an entire day with each of my imagined twins. In the morning I would take quite a while to choose my mate for the day. Had the man in the shining new fez glanced toward the window at my *chhhhss*? Yes? Then him today. This was not romance – I didn't want to become his wife. I *was* him: Mohammed, Joshkun, Turgut; I gave them all names. Sometimes we would walk to mosque with our prayer mat tucked beneath our arm. Sometimes we would write verses in the sunshine. Sometimes we would ogle young boys with our eyes and follow them into alleyways. We would walk out of town and never return. Sometimes we would come into the house and kill my an-ne and aunties.

70

I was the best boy in class. I memorized each chapter twice over. I was the most devout. I was Yaşar on my way to school, memorizing verses of the Qu'rān on my morning walk.

An-ne said I would become evil and idle standing at the window. She said this was my fate and women were meant to suffer because Eve herself was weak and thus were we all. Eve, she said, was close to Satan.

She lectured us constantly. A woman is always sinful, you must ask God's forgiveness. Repentance is obligatory – therefore, since God has demanded that we ask His forgiveness, we must have sinned. You have sinned. You must pray more than five times – keep God in your mind and speech, day and night. Your duty is to listen and to obey; you must never show your thoughts. Only listen. Only obey.

I imagined a rib that was not crooked when she spoke. I imagined it didn't need to be beaten straight.

I believed that I was the son. Somehow the angel had mistaken me for a girl. A simple mistake.

If An-ne had known my thoughts she would have whipped me more than she did. Perhaps she sensed my transgressions and that was why she slapped the bottoms of my feet longer and with greater vehemence.

In 1903, when An-ne lay on her deathbed, I was already eight years old. The women in the household wailed and beat themselves for days and nights, praying for her to recover. I remember how An-ne's white filmy eyes stared into mine, leaked onto her cheeks and into the bed sheets; she could not speak. Broken woman. I imagined for a moment her eyes asked for forgiveness. I squeezed her hand. I whispered softly into her ear: I am a boy.

My last memory of An-ne is of her widening eyes, of dark circles pressing against her dying vision like black hammers. If she could have removed her hand from mine, she would have.

I was married to Mustafa the reed-sharpener at thirteen. I begged my aunt to speak with Baba. All I knew of the reed-sharpener was his age: he was thirty-five when the wedding contract was signed. I had never met him, or even seen him, but for a thirteen-year-old girl, thirty-five was the age of a grandfather, not a husband. All I can recall from the day of our wedding ceremony is how his breath stank, how his few remaining teeth looked as if they'd cut me open.

An-ne and all the aunties used to say: a woman's responsibility is home, husband and children. Sons foremost. I became pregnant immediately and bore our first child, Timur, at fourteen. I had no idea at the time what was happening to me. When the child started moving inside of me I was terrified, sure that I had become possessed by a djinn. I tried to hide my belly from the other women in the household. One day my mother-in-law approached me and, slapping my cheeks, said, Stupid girl, stop your crying, you are too young to know.

In the first few months after my son was born, everyone was happy with me; Mustafa himself praised me and beat me less often for my transgressions.

The first years of marriage were filled with children. With the girls that came one after another it was life as usual in the household – scrambling so that there was enough food for the children and the men; succumbing to my husband's uninterrupted hands. Many days I ate next to nothing, an onion on a piece of bread. On the few occasions I saw one of my sisters they would gasp in shock. Maritsa, they'd say, you're disappearing before our eyes!

With so many responsibilities my imaginings ceased and I became a woman. I fed, I washed, I cooked and I cleaned. I worried. I never looked in the glass, but I knew I was becoming An-ne; I could feel my eyes begin to crevice like hers. My cheeks grew tight across the bones; I scolded the baby girls – Shut up. Never forget that you are meant to suffer. My memories of those times are of sick and hungry and crying children slapping at my knees when they could reach them. There were many of us in Mustafa's two-room family house, and I, of course, was the lowest of the women. We didn't know then that things would get unbearably worse. That the men would be taken into the army and starved to death, or die of disease, or stand shoeless on the cold snowy mountains of Russia. We didn't know that I would be the one to support the family.

But back then my mother-in-law ruled us all, and she reprimanded and berated me more than my mother once had.

What an easy life you have, Maritsa – such an un-appreciative girl.

You are careless and idle. You look like a whore.

You can do nothing well, Maritsa.

You are nothing, Maritsa.

In that house I could not even have a cup of tea without my mother-in-law's permission.

I prepared my items of toilette and I donned my çarsaf and asked my mother-in-law if I could accompany them to the hamam. She began to complain about me loudly, about my laziness, my demanding nature and huge appetite. I sat quietly and removed the veil. Eventually she gave me the money and we left the house, all of us together, and began our walk to the hamam.

I walked along behind my mother-in-law and the older women of the house. I can recall how my back ached that morning; my third daughter had brought on a constant pain which never left me. It was a day before Thursday, perhaps a Tuesday or a Monday. It was not so cold you needed woollen shirts and not so warm you longed to remove the heavy black çarsaf. The weather was wonderful, everyone said, one of God's blessed days. That morning I felt the pleasure of being outside of the house in the streets of the town. The rich men rode by us, sitting atop their mules, the boys walked to school with their teacher, the coffee-boy took his morning requests. The farmers who had come into town at dawn's light with their wares piled onto the oxen carts – I had heard the animals' laboured breathing and heavy steps before sunrise from the window on our street – had carved their impressions in the dirt road for me to admire. My pleasures were suspended intermittently by the body pains in my back, shoulders and feet, reminding me that life is suffering. For women, life is complete suffering.

We walked out of our neighbourhood and into the Armenian quarter, the women and our escort, Hasan, hurrying along at this point. A small infidel boy was in the street – except for him the streets were almost empty. The men were in their shops or offices and the children were in school. We all knew how the Christians sent their girls as well as their boys to be educated. This boy whom I hadn't noticed yet (I was still following the oxen's sculpted path) threw a rock against a building. It ricocheted and slammed into a window.

I looked up and saw the window shattering. It was as if the street stopped for a moment, as if I stopped also, or jerked sharply. The window broke piece by piece as I watched. I looked around me. I took in the sunshine, the autumn sky, the high three-storey houses, the fragrance of the air – cabbage, chickpeas, butter, onion and allspice – through the corners of my eyes and the slit in my veil. My mind started moving, like a lame horse it stumbled, confused it asked: why is this?

For a moment I could see myself from the vantage point of the rooftops, walking behind the women of the household and our escort, Hasan, a herd of women and a young man; a bent girl. How had I become a woman so easily? I was the boy, maligned by the mistake of an angel, or An-ne, wasn't I?

The infidel's rock snapped a rod inside me that day, and once broken there was no mending it.

The boy ran off as the Armenian lady of the house bent her head out of the window yelling at him. I'm not sure what she said; she spoke in their foreign gutturals. I noticed only how the lady's mouth worked itself open and closed like a bird; how her dark brown hair glinted in the muted light of day. I had never seen a woman hang her head from a window. I had so rarely seen a woman's hair in the yellow light of sun.

The lady looked at me for the briefest moment, our eyes ticked like marbles, our gazes hit and we both looked away immediately. Her eyes followed the movements of her body as she pulled back from the windowsill and closed the curtain; my eyes returned to the ground. I had seen fear in that look and also distaste. I wondered how a gâvur could find me distasteful. Wasn't she the polluted one? The vile one?

Chhhht, I heard the mother-in-law say. We all walked faster. But the walking changed nothing. The broken rod did not reform. Kings and princesses and ghosts began talking inside me from that day forward. They chewed on the broken pieces. Like bird bones.

American Consulate
Mamouret-ul-Aziz (Harput), Turkey
July 11, 1915

Honorable Henry H. Morgenthau,
American Ambassador,
Constantinople

Sir:

I have the honor to supplement my report of June 30 (File No. 840.1) in regard to the expulsion of the Armenians from this region, as follows:

On July 1 a great many people left and on July 3 several thousand more started from here. Others left on subsequent days. There is no way of obtaining figures but many thousand have already left. The departure of those living at Harput was postponed, however, and many women and children were allowed to remain temporarily. People began to hope that the worst was over and that those who remained might be left alone. Now it has been announced by the public crier that on Tuesday, July 13, every Armenian, without exception, must go.

If it were simply a matter of being obliged to leave here to go somewhere else it would not be so bad, but everyone knows it is a case of going to one's death. If there was any doubt about it, it has been removed by the arrival of a number of parties, aggregating several thousand people, from Erzurum and Erzincan. The first ones arrived a day or two after my last report was written. I have visited their encampment a number of times and talked with some of the people. A more pitiable sight cannot be imagined. They were almost without exception ragged, filthy, hungry and sick. That is not surprising in view of the fact that they have been on the road for nearly two months with no change of clothing, no chance to wash, no shelter and little to eat. The Government has been giving them some scanty rations here. I watched them one time when their food was brought. Wild animals could not be worse. They rushed upon the guards who carried the food and the guards beat them back with clubs, sometimes hitting hard enough to kill. To watch them one could hardly believe that these people were human beings.

As one walks through the camp mothers offer their children and beg one to take them. In fact, the Turks have been taking their choice of these children and girls for slaves, or worse. They have even had their doctors there to examine the more likely girls and thus secure the best ones.

There are very few men among them, as most have been killed on the road. All tell the same story of having been attacked and robbed by the Kurds. Most of them were attacked over and over again and a great many, especially the men, were killed. Women and children were also killed. Many died, of course, from sickness and exhaustion on the way and there have been deaths each day that they have been here. Several different parties have arrived and after remaining a day or two have been pushed on with no apparent destination. Those who have reached here are only a small portion, however, of those who started. By continuing to drive these people on in this way it will be possible to dispose of all of them in a comparatively short time.

The condition of these people indicates clearly the fate of those who have left and are about to leave from here. I believe nothing has been heard from any of them as yet, and probably very little will be heard. The system that is being followed seems to be to have bands of Kurds awaiting them on the road to kill the men especially and incidentally some of the others. The entire movement seems to be the most thoroughly organized and effective massacre this country has ever seen.

Not many men have been spared, however, to accompany those who are being sent into exile, for a more prompt and sure method has been used to dispose of them. Several thousand Armenian men have been arrested during the past few weeks and put in prison. Many hundreds at a time were rounded up in that way during the night.

All Armenian soldiers have, in the same manner, been arrested and confined in a building at one end of the town. No distinction has been made between those who have paid their military exemption tax and those who have not. Their money was accepted and they were arrested and sent off with the others. It was said that they were to go somewhere to work on the roads but no one has heard from them and that is undoubtedly false.

There seems to be a definite plan to dispose of all the Armenian men, but after the departure of the families, during the first few days of the enforcement of the order, it was announced that women and children with no men in the family might remain here for the present and many hoped that the worst was over. The American missionaries began considering plans to aid the women and children who would be left here with no means of support. It was thought that perhaps an orphanage could be opened to care for some of the children, especially those who had been born in America and then brought here by their parents, and also those who belonged to parents connected in some way with the American Mission and schools. I went to see the Vali about this matter yesterday and was met with a flat refusal. He said we could aid these people if we wished to do so, but the Government was establishing orphanages for the children and we could not undertake any work of that nature. An hour after I left the Vali the announcement was made that all the Armenians remaining here, including women and children must leave on July 13.

The evident plan of the Government is to give no opportunity for any educational or religious work to be done here by foreign missionaries. Some Armenian women will be taken as Muslim wives and some children will be brought up as Muslims, but none of them will be allowed to come under foreign influences. The country is to be purely Muslim and nothing else.

Some of the missionaries think they would like to remain here and try to work among Muslims. I not only think it would be very dangerous for them to undertake it but do not believe they will be allowed to do anything along that line. I shall not be surprised, as I have said before, if all the American missionaries are ordered to leave here in the near future. I do not think for a moment that they will be allowed to open any of the schools again and it's quite probable also that both the school and the hospital buildings may be seized by the Government. It seems certain that there will not be any work for them to do here, nor will they be permitted to do any work.

The effect industrially and commercially of the expulsion of the Armenians from this region will be to throw it back to the Middle Ages. It is officially stated that ninety percent of the trade and of the business carried on through the banks is that of Armenians. Business of all kinds will now be destroyed beyond the possibility of its ever being restored. In some trades there will be no mechanics or workmen at all. It is difficult to understand how those Turks who have had any taste of civilization will be able to live unless exceptions are made and there does not seem to be any indication of that. There will be no banks, no Christian schools, no Christian churches. With one stroke the country is set back two to three hundred years. The same will be true of Diyarbakir and all other parts of this consular district.

Mr Davis, sir.

Yes, Cavass Garabed?

The gentlemen arrive for the bridge game, sir. The Vali Sabit Bey is at the front gate with his escort.

Yes, yes. It's gotten quite late, hasn't it? I'll have to finish these reports later.

Thrushes

He stays for a moment staring up at the ceiling in the morning darkness. He unbuckles his legs and stretches them out long like a band of flat ribbon pulled taut. He twists his head to the left and then the right. His left ankle clicks when he turns it slowly. He lifts the sheet and spun-wool quilt from his body, creating a warm tunnel. He smells their excreta on the cotton, the oil from her hair. In the darkness he imagines the rise and fall of her body like a man remembering a hill he has climbed or a footpath he has taken: the smooth backs of her thighs, her rough heel, the depression at the base of her spine, the notches in her back rising from her skin like birds pushing against a canvas tent. Their scent rises from the bed like a scurry of thrushes from a tunnel, making him smile for the first time in months.

He places his feet into his leather house shoes; he lights the kerosene lamp and covers himself with the striped ochre and cream silken robe the Vali gave him months ago. He walks to the dresser and peers at himself in the hanging oval mirror. He reaches into the bowl of fresh water with both of his hands. He looks into his blue eyes, which are brown in the early-morning dimness. He splashes water onto his face. The water gathers in his thick eyebrows.

How does a person look contented?

He makes a map of Lucine's body. He Xs pink-brown nipples, her closed navel; he draws a straight line from her chest bone to her pubis. His mouth follows his demarcations. Degenerate, he whispers to his reflection and arching, dripping brows. He picks up the washcloth that rests by the bowl of water and wets it; he wipes each of his armpits, his loose chest muscles. He lifts his fallow genitals. He cups his penis in his hand and gently pulls the foreskin back. He washes thoroughly.

The sunlight enters through the window at his back. He looks again into the glass and sees shades of himself in the oval mirror. A man with thick brown-grey brows, chapped skin, transparent eyes. His appearance surprises him – he looks different from the man he perceives himself to be. The Ivy League man. The son of Long Island's north shore. He wears a silk robe, water drips down his face, he has pulled the foreskin of his penis tight. He is smiling.

Who are you? he whispers. There is a strange feeling in his chest, like small birds rushing out.

Lucine taps softly on the door.

Your breakfast, sir.

Enter please.

She opens the door and moves into the bedroom bearing a tray of coffee and bread with string cheese. She places the tray on the round table by the window as she always does.

82

Davis is standing before the mirror, tying his cravat. He looks at her as she lifts the cup of coffee and plate of food from the tray and places them on the table.

Lucy, come here.

She tucks the tray beneath her arm and walks towards him. Davis buttons his suit jacket. She stands behind him. He stares at the reflection of Lucine, hair uncovered as he prefers it when they are alone.

How is your brother faring?

Well, sir. He is relieved by the medicines.

That's good news. I'm well today. And you? Are you well, today?

Yes, sir, I am well.

Are you very busy? He presses his hands down his suit jacket.

Yes. There is much to be done in the kitchen.

Lucy. Lucy. He smiles into the mirror. *Merci* . . . my dear. *Merci*.

Sir, the children require breakfast.

My dear, of course.

Daughter of Setrak the Dentist, and Wife to Elia, a Drug Store Pharmacist

In this world the roots of the trees climb skyward, seeking blind sustenance. Their roots like beggars crawl along the gutters, ascend the walls of houses, enter first-storey windows – devouring, they leave through the attic window taking the hiding men in women's dress from the closed cupboards and wooden trunks, they tip them like joy onto the streets so that the police can easily collect and decapitate, disembowel, and place the lonely severed heads on the centre-square pikes for viewing. I have seen these unseeing bundles staring ruthlessly. They have followed me as I made my way across the town square. Their black eyes speak to me. Sister, they say, Auntie, tell me what has become of *me*? Levon, Bedros, Hovannes, Armen – I repeat their names so that they will know I've heard them, these unmade men; heads lined up in a row on wooden poles.

The rests of men are buried amidst the tree branches, suffocated below the earth. Their fingers grasp children's songs, holy beads; the imprint of wedding bands is etched on the ring fingers, like a carving of a boy's name on the trunk of an oak. There is company and adornment for the branches below ground: crenated leaves, pressed thorns, stifled buds, bundles of men.

The sun has descended, and if it shines, here we can no longer tell of it. The roots require night darkness, like soil. We live now as rodents; blind, we hear everything. We hear men think. We hear their decisions and their concern with their heavy bowels; their desires for violating and eating.

Some of us have left our children on strange doorsteps. Some of us have bartered in the darkness. Some have unmade children.

Everything is exchangeable. Detachable. For us, for the women, it is considered improper to buy and sell.

There is a man who writes letters day after day, telegrams, reports, long pages of notes. He writes continuously in the mornings, in this darkness which he does not perceive, the lamps illuminated, his tea and snacks when he wishes it. On Wednesday evenings he plays bridge with the Commander of the XI Army Corps and his personal friend, the Vali. I serve them carefully, my head covered and tipped to the floor, my steps light and small, my hating like breath.

I reserve my voice with this man. I dole out words sparingly, like a frugal peasant woman; I understand that each word is a parcel of me. I give him *Yes* and *Mister* in his own language. In mine, with my soft breath like my light steps, I tell him: blind blind blind. To me he is like a woman, or worse. He preens in front of the mirror. I have seen it from the corner of the room as I set down his breakfast. He is weak like a woman; he is gullible and stupid. Sometimes I have the slightest shame for the Amerigatsi. He does not speak our Oriental languages. They make jokes about him when he is in the room. Donkey farter, Chief Diplomat of the Pussy-Kitties, they laugh. Mr Davis smiles brightly and nods to them: *C'est votre tour, Monsieur Sabit Bey*. He is the mouse the Turkish authorities bat between their paws, a toy for them, a joy on the streets.

He rides out on his horse when he can and returns saddened and in disgust. I know that beneath his smile and sympathy eyes he thinks of us as animals, no better than dogs. He asks me, How can I help you and your brother? and I see past his words behind the breath, into the pupils, and behind those also. The question is, How did your people end up like this, no better than dogs?

I pleaded with him one time. I used my tongue and my school words: *My brother to America. My brother to America. My brother to America.*

He turned his face from me and looked towards the hanging mirror; he turned his face back to mine. He touched himself beneath the bed sheets. Yes, he said, touching me. I understood that giving him my words was a betrayal.

My five-year-old brother has eyes like his sister and the hands of his father. He sleeps with the other boys on the second floor. I have trained him well. Before we came to the American Consul's house, I taught him: Lucine, Lucine, Lucine. If he called me differently I slapped him, I beat him with my shoes. He bruised and scabbed, this little boy. I beat his mother out of him and a sister into him. Heel marks on his face and arms like birthmarks.

The other ladies here believe they know everything. The boy, the Consul. We cook together in the big kitchen. We cook for the people Mr Davis has counted, and we cook for the others who hide in the stable, next to the wall, beneath the trees. We sift and we wash, we pound and boil. They do not speak to me directly. Theirs is another hatred.

This girl thinks she's better than us.

This girl would have been put on the street in other times.

This girl is a shame to our race.

This girl has no pride.

This girl, look how she walks, as if she's a princess.

This girl, she's lazy.

This girl will suffer the wrath of God.

They do not say worse things in front of me. Whore. Sodom and Gomorrah. These things they say when I leave the room.

This is the inside-out world. The black side. The devil's world. I cannot recall if there has ever been a place different from this one; a time of a different velocity. Here the days have no beginning, there is no rising sun to mark them. Each day is endless, each day is the night. The dark root night. Devouring us.

Mardiros

❧

The Commander called him Mardiros while pissing on his face and buttocks. Or at least that was what he thought they said. His ears were clogged that morning from a bad head cold; the stinging of his cuts and burns, he admitted to himself, was also a distraction.

When the police had finished the interrogation they lifted him up in their arms towards the ceiling. Mardiros felt a breeze flutter across his chest, down the line of his stomach onto the place where his testicles had once been.

I feel lighter now, he said, without all that hair to weigh me down.

The police bounced him up in their arms in agreement. A small shard of plaster of Paris fell onto his leg from the moulding on the ceiling and Mardiros knew it was a sign from Newgod. His baptismal ceremony complete, the police dragged him back to his cell in chains. The hairs that had been plucked from his beard and moustache stuck to his skin; pus was an unexpectedly fine adhesive. Mardiros smiled and recited the Newourfather.

When the police released him the following week by dumping him in a naked heap next to the other recently liberated inmates in the ditch four miles from town, Mardiros became dead like the rest of his cohorts and he waited for the Newresurrection. He waited on the heap for three days. Soon he noticed that bits and pieces of the congregation were departing in the mouths of birds of prey, rats, wolves and hyenas. He asked Newgod: What made you forget me, Effendi Bey? Mardiros pondered and reviewed the lesson he knew the Newgod was teaching him until finally he came upon an answer: I must return to town.

At dawn Mardiros rose and began his trek back to Kharphert. His feet ached when the dust and rocks and thorny bushes became lodged in the one-and-a-half-inch openings in his soles, but soon he became accustomed to it and his feet and the dust and the pebbles and the thorns became one, like a humanshoe. When Mardiros reached the base of the hill leading up to town, he looked up to the sky and said, Newgod, grant me another sign.

He waited and waited in that position until the flies got comfortable in the sores on his neck, back, and buttocks. When the flies settled in for a good long wait and their eggs hatched and the maggots did their work, eating the dead flesh in his wounds, Mardiros genuflected and made the sign of a straight line, straight to Newgod. *Merci*, he said, and began climbing the hill.

After Mardiros reached the edge of town he stopped to consider if he should head towards the Armenian quarter or to the army headquarters. Where can I do my best work? he wondered. As he stood there, he noticed two Armenian hags approaching him. They both wore the black çarsaf and bent their heads in supplication. They were crying softly as they walked. When they came so close that he could touch them, Mardiros stopped them with his right hand.

Ladies, why are you crying?

The men have all been taken. There are only boys under eight years of age left to us.

Look at my bare chest and feet, touch and see me. I am a man above the age of eight. Do you have anything to eat?

Only raw cabbage leaves; they may give you gas, the lady on the left said.

Boiled anise is good for gas, suggested the lady on the right, and she handed Mardiros a full and limp light green leaf of cabbage. He took it and ate it slowly.

Ladies, he said, I am proof that the men have not been murdered. They are four miles from here in a big heap, not too far from the lake. Even as we speak, they are being hawks, vultures, fieldmice, rats, flies, queen ants, millipedes and hyenas. They have done their suffering, he said, and the pus from his sores dripped onto his feet and the earth around him, leaving a ring like a halo in the dirt. The maggots lifted their heads for the sermon.

They are rising into the living. Our men will be the reason we have a fine harvest this year. The dolma will be abundant.

The two Armenian women fell to their knees in joy and moved to wash and kiss Mardiros' feet. They noticed the swollen and decrepit and missing pieces of his lower extremities. The nails missing from his toes.

What happened to the toes on this foot? asked the lady on the left to the lady on the right beneath her breath. They shook their heads in unison and created a newritual: they smoothed and patted the ground around the halo of his present and missing toes. Mardiros touched them on the head and said, Stay here in this town, and blessed them. The two hags then continued on their way.

Mardiros decided to walk to the army headquarters and speak with the prophets there. As he approached the building that the army had requisitioned only one month earlier (before that it had been the Armenian School for Boys, established 1886), he felt a twinge in his right hand and looked down to see a small rat dangling from his pinkie. As he watched, it gnawed off the smallest digit at the root of his hand, then jumped to the ground and scurried away. The finger vied in weight and size with the rodent's own body mass and dimensions. It must be a newsign, Mardiros said aloud.

The guard who saw Mardiros approaching smiled a welcome and opened the gates to him.

Good to see you again.

Yes, I'm glad to be back. I still have several unanswered questions.

The Commander is waiting in the usual place. Go right in.

Mardiros made for the room at the back of the building that he knew so well. He walked down the quiet corridor. Where's the usual hullabaloo? he wondered. When he arrived at the red door he opened it slowly and stepped inside. The room was immaculate except for a few hairs left in corners and in the cracks and hinges of things. The floor had been mopped. The Commander sat in his stately chair.

Mardiros, my son. How are you?

I'm fine, fine. Just fine, sir. But I have a question, effendi.

Yes, yes, anything. The Commander smiled brightly and scratched his balls three times. He shifted his cock to a more comfortable position within his loose Turkish-style trousers.

Mardiros approached the large chair and hunched down in front of it. What happens after this story? he said, looking between the chief's splayed legs.

Agh. Don't worry, my son. This story will never have happened after it's finished.

And the rumours, where will they go?

The Commander adjusted himself again. With the marchers – the Mesopotamian has space enough for everything.

You've thought of everything, sir.

Yes. We thought of you also.

And three apples fell from heaven, one for the storyteller, one for the listener, and one for the eaves-dropper.

Baba

ↄ⌀⅋⅋ↄↄ⅋

Hagop sits upon his sleeping pallet and ties his left shoe. He has the custom of always putting his left shoe on first, a habit which developed from a small superstition he held as a boy (left shoe first is an auspicious beginning for a day) and tonight is no different; he puts the right shoe on and ties it. Later, when the gendarmes pound their wooden rifle butts on the front door of his home, he is fully dressed in his black suit and seated in the salon with Yughaper. He hears the voices of the police at the ground-floor entrance. Open it! they say.

When Hagop stands up from where he has been seated on the divan, he feels a few loose strands of his wife's hair brush against his jaw and neck. Yughaper sits beside him wrapped in an embroidered shawl and she stares at his rising back while the noise in the street intensifies. He rubs the spot where the hairs touched him. They have listened to the ruckus in the quarter for hours, and although they clearly heard the one-two-threes of wooden stocks on wooden doors and shutters as the police claimed entry into homes on other streets, it was not until the rifle butts slammed against their own portal that the commotion became true and palpable to them – a thing which fully dried the spit in their mouths, a din that aped the booming in their chests. *Tell me*, *what have I done*? *Where are you taking him*? The questions that had been called out endlessly from the doorways that night, became their own.

Hagop turns his head for a moment as he passes through the doorway of the first-floor salon and he looks back at his wife, at the woman he has known since he was a boy. As he looks at her in the glow of the kerosene lamp, at her thick brown hair tied haphazardly at the nape, at her long day dress, and at her dark eyes which seem to darken more as he stares intently, he suddenly sees her running from him as she did when they were children, when he and his friends used to tease her and rain the mulberries down upon her head by shaking the tree branches.

You will be sorry for this, Hagop Demirdjian, the seven-year-old Yughaper used to say. Do not forget that the Lord says all things require their payment.

He won't make me pay, he used to goad her. God prefers boys.

For a moment Hagop can see the two Yughapers simultaneously and distinctly: the girl from childhood gazing up at him from below the mulberry tree, a spray of red berries tucked into her braids – and the wife of fifteen years, staring momentarily into his eyes and then moving her gaze to his lapel. His kaleidoscopic vision is a beautiful form. And he notices a tight tenderness in his chest then, and for a man unaccustomed to this tightness it is an odd feeling, an affection he had not claimed in his life of duty and labour. His vision an unexpected epiphany.

Hagop shifts his gaze from Yughaper to the hanging lamps.

Wife, be careful dispensing the gold lira.

He then turns his back to her. He moves from the doorway toward the stairwell and he stops momentarily. He turns and enters the salon again and as he approaches Yughaper, he removes his wedding band from his left hand. He places his gold wedding band by her side on the divan and he turns and goes through the doorway and down the stairs to unlatch the front door.

Hagop pulls open the door leading to the street and he is roughly cuffed on the cheek with a rifle butt. He stumbles momentarily and then regains his balance. He looks up and sees three young gendarmes before him; he touches his front incisor with his tongue and feels a sharp triangle where his slippery tooth had been.

I dislike waiting one minute for a dog.

There's only one in this house.

The gendarme at the rear makes a mark in his book and then turns and walks toward the residence next door.

The two remaining men enter the house and, laying their hands on Hagop, turn him around so that he faces the passageway leading towards the kitchen. While one gendarme holds him, the other pulls his arms behind his back. The policeman begins to tie Hagop's wrists together tightly with thick rope.

I'm getting better at this, Ilhan. Quicker.

Hagop observes the machinations of the knotting in the moving shapes of the shadows projected onto the wall; he swallows a crack of tooth and a chaw of mucus and blood.

The gendarmes turn Hagop round again to face the

street entrance to the house and begin pushing him out the front door. Yughaper steps from the kitchen into the passageway, dressed now in a dark çarsaf. She sees the back of Hagop's disappearing head and the cuffs of his trousers. Just as the front door swings shut, Yughaper feels a heat behind her.

Baba told you to stay with your brothers and sister.

Yughaper sits down where she has been standing and she digs her fingers into the hair at her crown. Anaguil stands behind her mother, dressed in her nightclothes and a shawl. She clenches her arms around her body and presses her hands into fists across her tight ribs.

When the knife clanks to the floor by Yughaper's feet, the mother doesn't raise her eyes in question to her daughter; she doesn't ask Anaguil what exactly she meant to do with a paring knife. Yughaper picks up the small knife by its blade and, wrapping her hand around it, tucks the knife into the sleeve of the long veil. Then she lifts her hand to her forehead again, clenching her hair. Lines of blood begin to dribble into her eyes, darkening her vision.

Once in the street, in the busy night, Hagop joins the other bound men. Although he can hardly see them he can feel them. He hears their heavy breathing and it reminds him of the field oxen. The gendarmes begin tying the men together in groups of four and the Armenians say nothing. They have quickly learned from the loquacious men – the men who have had an ear or hand removed with clean dispatch – to remain silent. Those men stand mute now in the street while pools of blood gather in their shoes or drip onto their bare feet.

The old man Gaspar Magdassarian is the last man on the street to come ssss-ing and ssssa-ing from his house, pulling on the ropes with his two hands. Undeterred by the quiet, he asks the policemen, But why this? Why now?

A young gendarme, a boy with no facial hair, turns and pushes the end of his bayonet into the man's belly, spilling the old man's viscera onto the street.

You understand now, effendi?

The young policeman wipes his blade clean on the dead man's shirt-tail. Gaspar Magdassarian's body is left where it has fallen and the bound men are ordered to begin walking to the police station. As Hagop steps over the old man, the bootmaker, a stray uncontrolled thought runs through his mind: perhaps bootmaker-Gaspar will be the luckiest man tonight.

As they walk the half-mile to the commissary which is also the townhall and the town jail, the moon shines three-quarters full. Occasionally a cloud passes across its face, leaving the men in complete darkness so that momentarily they become like strange djinn to each other. When the moon's light is once again uncovered the men can see their feet and the shadows of their heads and arms, they can recognize the visage of their neighbour or backgammon partner or the butcher who always gives them the choicest cut of lamb; they see the face of the man who they argued with last week over the price of a mule.

Hagop gazes at his feet as he walks and stumbles when the man to his left or right jerks him. The man at his left side turns his head toward him, panting, and Hagop thinks how his breath smells like an old dog's. As Hagop stares at his feet, sometimes seeing his boots and sometimes not, depending upon the whims of the air currents and the clouds and the moonlight, he imagines himself like a rift of loose wind. He envisions loosening himself from the ropes and sailing into the dark night and out onto the darker plains, like a lonesome ship.

If he listens closely in the night he believes he can hear the whisperings of men – not of the bound men who stand at his side, but of the Armenian men who have haunted these valleys and plateaux and plains for centuries. He thinks he can hear their handless spirits saying to him in the spring night, Brother, do you believe a few thousand years of history make any difference to armed men?

Sweetness on the Tongue

We'll purchase a tin of honey on our way to the meydan.

They veer down a side street and stop at a small and dim stall. The main bazaar is still some distance away.

Eh, whatya want then?

The Turkish vendor gets up from his stool behind the wooden table. Yughaper reaches beneath the black veiled robe and searches for her coins. She holds her hand with the money out to the old man. He inhales deeply, the air whistling through the gaps in his row of upper teeth.

A large tin of honey, effendi. Low-grade is fine.

A large tin of low-grade, eh? Fifty paras.

I have forty. Here. Here is forty.

Fifty or nothing.

Your low-grade honey is the colour of gold today, effendi?

Yes, madam, prices have risen. These are difficult times.

Forty-five, then. Forty-five.

The merchant grins.

Forty-five, then.

He reaches behind to the wooden shelves and retrieves the rusted metal tin.

Please, effendi, can you open the honey tin?

The Turkish merchant stares at Yughaper and Anaguil for a moment. He smiles again and sucks his teeth, whistling.

Anaguil and Yughaper head directly to the centre of town. As they walk towards the jail, Yughaper reaches underneath her çarsaf as if to adjust her clothing or rub her abdomen.

You will give this to Baba.

She hands the tin of honey to Anaguil.

When they arrive at the jail the mother and daughter pass through a large wooden door and down a long corridor until they come to an open patio where there are a few tables and chairs scattered about. Five gendarmes sit smoking and drinking milk-white raku. Their rifles lean against the backs of their chairs. Across the courtyard two barred windows reveal the contained and packed men on the other side of the cement walls. Groups of women, all dressed in the black çarsaf, huddle near the walls; they clasp their children's hands. They softly murmur their prayers.

We'll be home soon enough.

It's finished.

Whose fault is this?

The Church. They said, Absolute obedience to the government orders.

Shut up, boy. It's the intellectuals like you in the

capital who started all of this business. *We can be released from the Turkish yoke yet,* you said.

We said *reform*, Mr Ignatosian, we did not say rebellion. We said: equality for the millets, just as they'd promised us in 1908 in the new constitution. We said: freedom from extortion, massacre, pillaging.

Shut up the both of you and let me rest.

My hands have turned an unfamiliar colour.

You're telling me you can still feel them?

Don't push me.

You've the breath of a donkey.

I never should have come for a visit. My mother begged me for two years to return and find a good wife. What kind of husband will I be now? A corpse cannot seed his fields in Michigan.

Where will they take us?

To a ditch.

Maybe this is, as they say, a formality. Maybe we'll have uniforms soon and go to the front.

I could not kill another Armenian man, Rus or no.

Don't talk, you idiot. It's idiots like you who they've used to justify this business. For years they sought a solution to their 'Armenian Question', and here it is, gentlemen. Your American gold teeth and city shoes don't mean anything here, Coin-seller-Yervant.

It is the not-knowing that cages a man.

It's not being able to take a shit without four men having to accompany you and three hundred watching you that enrages a man.

You have always been an uncouth and vulgar man, Ash-collector-Hamazasp.

If they'd untie these ropes we'd have a chance.

What will happen to my three boys?

I am a rich man. I know the Vali personally. This

is a mistake. Tell them Bakrat Gregorian is here. By mistake.

Where is God's justice?

We'll fight in the war and then we'll be home soon enough.

My wife gives birth next month. It's our first child.

Who will mind the pharmacy?

It's all lies.

Who is keeping the ovens warm?

Fooroonjee-Harutiun, your bread is the least of our problems.

We are the pawn in this war game.

. . . the payment.

. . .

. . .

. . .

All is unknown.

It's finished.

Get up, you three. I must piss.

It's you intellectuals in Constantinople who started all of this business. You richboys who went to study in France and England. We're all together now. There's no difference *now*, is there, smartboy?

You stink. I can smell your fear.

I'm a rich man. I know the Vali personally. He comes to my house for tea. Tell them Bakrat Gregorian the silk merchant is here. By mistake.

Uf.

Yughaper and Anaguil approach the group of soldiers slowly. The women and children huddle together in a dark mass.

I've brought my husband some honey.

She holds out a gold lira.

The captain does not look up from his card game. He nods to another policeman, who gets up and walks over to Yughaper. The younger gendarme stares at her bent head and modest Muslim attire. He takes the gold coin, letting his hand linger for a moment on Yughaper's palm. When he feels her tremble he switches his gaze to Anaguil and holds out his hand: he will have some of the sweet poppy honey. Anaguil stares at his extended hand, at the knuckles covered in short white scars like silver filigree. She hands him the tin. She turns and wanders over to one of the two windows facing into the open-air jail.

I'm looking for Hagop, Berj and Hratch, sons of Kevork Demirdjian.

The word passes quickly among the men and it is only moments before her father and Amo Berj and Amo Hratch appear with the men they are still bound to. Her father's eyes are dark in the slanted sun.

Anaguil, you look like a puffed black hen in that dress.

Baba. Are you well? Have you eaten Mama's food that we sent? Baba, are you warm enough at night?

Iyo.

Get the two bitches who brought the honey.

Anaguil snaps her head around and she sees a flash of metal flying through the air, glittering like water pools.

Shud! Join the women, daughter.

Find the bitch infidels.

Shud!

Shud!

Anaguil moves quickly in her long black veil into the large group of women. The knife continues its trajectory, flying through the morning blue sky, brilliant. It strikes a wall on the far side of the courtyard and drops to the ground. Its handle cracks and breaks in two from the impact. Honey shines on the blade.

The young soldier with the scarred knuckles holds his right hand high in the air. The blood drips down his palm.

I've sliced my fingers in two from their trickery.

There in the crowd of women Anaguil finds her mother staring intently at the stone floor of the courtyard. The other women close in around them, shielding them. The guards begin pressing at the circle. The women and small children who are bound together by their black vestments become like one dark animal herd. The guards strike the women standing on the periphery, they beat them on their heads and backs, they slap their cheeks.

Where's the bitch and her infidel pup?

. . . for the Lord is for you.

Cut off their hands.

Slice off their tits.

Eh bitches, come out, come out.

Sshhtt. Sshhtt.

. . . do not bring us to the time of trial . . .

Armenian infidel whore, you'll soon feel the glory of our nation between your legs.

The men in the jail strain at the two barred windows. Their foreheads press to the confining metal, their hands pull on the bindings, the rope saws at their torn flesh.

Sshhtt. Sshhtt.

Sshhtt. Sshhtt.

*   *   *

104

The policemen give up their sport of finding the woman and the girl in a pitch sea of women and girls and boy children, and they sit back down at their tables to resume the card game and the laughter and the drinks of milk-white raku. They understand that too much time spent looking for a woman is a loss of face and dignity.

Jumhur, maybe your an-ne can clean up your cuts for you!

Ja ja.

Or maybe you can pay the new girl, Maritsa, to make it feel better.

She makes me feel better, Jumhur!

Whose deal?

In time Anaguil and Yughaper slip out of the government building and head towards home. Neither looks back towards the jail. Anaguil looks at her mother, who stares straight ahead. Beyond the horizon.

They walk briskly past the closed windows and covered openings, past the locked doors. A fierce quiet hangs on the streets of the quarter like clear ribbons, entangling them.

The Lion-Hearted

ഷ്ട്ര

That particular afternoon in Professor Najarian's
orchard, as the neighbourhood boys lay on the soft
grass and gazed at the blue summer skies, Karnik stood
above them in his impersonation of the broken and
pitiable King Lear.

Why should a dog, a horse, a rat, he recited in the
English while shaking his hands towards the plum
tree, and then deciding for good measure to include
the local fauna, a goat or a louse, have life, And thou
no breath at all?

He twisted his head from side to side vehemently,
yelling out into the still air on a long and deep breath.
Nevernevernevernevernevernevernever, as the boys
began to laugh.

Karnik's mother, Digin Hassig, came running out of
the house when she heard the ruckus, thinking that
the boys were fighting.

She saw her son with his fists raised to heaven and
she yelled out over his nevers, Uf! Keep that foreign
nonsense down! and returned to the house to continue her cooking. The other boys, who had jumped

up when Digin Hassig came outside, smiled slyly, and repeating after Karnik in soft voices began: Nay-verrr, nay-verrr, nay-verrrrr! and then immediately fell to pummelling each other on the back and shoulders.

Unlike the adults in the quarter who found Karnik's behaviour odd, the children thought that his ramblings in alien tongues were wonderful. They did not reprove his proclivity for breaking out into long-winded recitations of Shakespeare or Baudelaire or Sophocles (with small additions or addenda in Armenian to convey the general plot or to improve upon a weak line). And Karnik's frequent invitations to share the plums and apricots and figs in his family's orchard, and his ability to shoot a marble more deftly and cleanly than any boy within a mile radius, only added to his popularity among the juvenile population of Kharphert's Armenian quarter.

Karnik's father, Professor Najarian, had given courses in history and philology at Euphrates College since 1898. He was a gentleman fascinated not only by the course of human events and their articulation in writing, but with the vast mysteries of life he could fathom in the smallest things: naturally occurring and man-made.

Karnik, he would say to his only son as he cuddled him on his lap, there is a reason for everything. We must look for the reasons. That is why you are my Karnik – you must be fearless, my boy.

The professor, known affectionately in the coffee-house as The Man of Letters and Putters, spent his free time pursuing his unending studies of the cosmos, seeking his answers in a series of experiments and agitations.

In the West it is the time of Great Inventions but what of the professor of Philology and History in the East? What of the man who lives on the old silk road which once extended from China to Baghdad?

For a man educated at the Royal University of Würzburg, physics was a border-free enterprise, one not only for the trained physicist or doctor, but also for the inquisitive tinkerer − for any educated man of letters. Professor Najarian regularly exchanged correspondence with his friends and colleagues in Germany, the men he had befriended when he pursued his studies at the end of the last century.

While reading a paper by Mr Wilhem Conrad during a winter recess, Professor Najarian noticed his wife had a chest cold she could not shake. Digin Hassig hacked and wheezed through much of the season's festivities, until finally the professor, looking up from his reading of the treatise in the salon, decided that he must ascertain the contents of such a maleficent and noise-making chest cavity. And so he returned to his notion that well-laid ideas could be transmuted and made physical.

The professor raised himself from the divan and went to work in the second-storey room. He dragged his papers out and pulled his English chair up to a small wooden table in his laboratory and began to assemble parts: a gas discharge tube and a Ruhmkorff coil, and mumbling out loud (in German, an inventor's tongue) began his thinking and his tinkering. When Digin Hassig called him to dinner that evening he didn't lift his head from his work. When Karnik entered the laboratory he didn't hear him, and when his son tapped him on the shoulder and whispered, *Papa, c'est trop tard*. Early in bed and early riseup make a man contented and wise, the professor simply ruffled his son's hair and shooed him out the door without praising the boy's latest linguistic achievements.

Digin Hassig clipped her son on the head when he returned to the salon scratching his chin and staring at the floor. She had sent the boy up to the second floor to bring her husband out of his concentration, knowing him as she did and knowing that if he began in earnest he could be ensconced on the second floor for weeks on end – as he had the previous winter for three and a half weeks, making his wife and daughters worry tremendously when he refused to eat meat and anything cooked or salted. When he had insisted on eating a full head of garlic each day.

Garlic is good for the circulation and it clears the mind. Cooking things, on the other hand, interferes with the machinations of the cerebrum, the blood flows, and its attribute flatulence is wholly unredeemed, eh-eh.

When the professor finally descended to the first storey the previous winter and sat down to dinner as if nothing strange had transpired and began to eat the chicken and yogurt soup, his wife and daughters covered their mouths with their hands. Karnik stuck both his index fingers into his nostrils and pursed his lips; he thought of the dog corpse he had once discovered in an alleyway with the maggots running in and out of the eye sockets and the fur of the dog that when nudged with a stick fell off like snow from a tree branch.

The professor's newly grown beard covered his cheeks and neck and crept down onto his chest, making the hair on his body and face twist together like grapevines on the bower. His eyes were no longer dark brown but crimson like glassy pomegranate seeds. He had lost so much weight that his pants, even with his belt on its tightest notch, slipped to below his hips, making them look not at all like European wear, but the traditional Turkish baggy trouser. The professor ate the soup slowly and then wiped a drop of broth from his upper lip daintily with a napkin, missing the liquid that still glistened on his chin hairs. The table was quiet and the others tried to force themselves to eat despite the stench. As the second course was served the smell began to intensify and to wrap itself around each diner like an afternoon breeze in the deepest heat of the day. It crawled into each family member's nostrils (except Karnik's, who continued to plug his nose without any verbal rebuke from his father and only recriminatory glances from his mother and sisters) and kept itself there like an uninvited lodger, so that each time the women breathed in they tasted in the back of their mouths (the unwanted guest having moved down their throats) some of the results of their husband and father's attempt to make the world of ideas into a tangible and physical *thing*.

When the meal finished the professor pushed himself up from his chair and sauntered into the salon to roll a cigarette. The three daughters – Lisabeth, Mary and Melane – dashed to the lavatory and fought over who could enter first. Mary, being the heaviest of the three, pushed her way past her sisters to the commode and Melane settled for the wash basin. Lisabeth, with despair in her heart and a rolling stomach, a stomach that now squeezed and tightened her insides like a washerwoman does with the wet linen, turned her head to the side and sank to the tiled hallway and retched onto the shininess of the brown tiles.

Afterwards, feeling relieved, she was amazed with the colours and textures of her own spewn meal: light greens, browns of every shade, white seeds and a bright sunny yellow like the yolk from an egg.

During that particular hiatus in the laboratory, or 'Sinkhole' as the women of the house secretly referred to it, the professor worked out a way to listen from long distances. The following afternoon, cleaned and clean-smelling, in a dark blue suit, The Man of Letters and Putters hauled his wife to church.

He dragged her, surprised and taken aback, to St Vartan's on a Tuesday afternoon. Upon entering the holy house, he forced her down the nave. The professor climbed up to the stained-glass window of the Virgin Mary and attached two wires to the Virgin's upturned visage, while Digin Hassig grumbled underneath her breath all the while and wondered to herself if the same foreign tongues which had corrupted her husband's mind were also destroying her son's. The professor referred to his notes in the original German and tutted and commanded the contraption he had towed along with his wife into the nave to *be sure to do something*. Then he commanded his wife to stay put at all costs and not to move an inch! at all costs and then he ordered her to sing and to sing continuously until he returned. Knowing that under all circumstances a wife must obey her husband, she began with the Morning Prayer.

As he was leaving the church, the professor raised his hand into the air and yelled out, *Ich kann das machen*! and his pants, precariously balanced with a tightened-all-the-way belt that was now not tight enough, slipped to his knees like a penitent sinner. Digin Hassig raised her voice an octave when she caught sight of her husband's undergarments and the professor, nonplussed for a moment, hoped this was not a bad sign. He quickly regained his sense of purpose, pulled his pants up and ran out the door and across the street, trailing long wires in his wake.

He ran towards the coffee-house across from the church and, after paying two boys outside to make sure nobody stepped on the black wires, entered the smoky coffee-house shouting, Friends! Brothers! Listen to the song of God! He held up the small metal cup with the black wires attached and shushed all of the men in the coffee-house. The men, accustomed to Putterer Bey's yearly discoveries, quieted and then heard, softly and dimly, and roughly like a woman talking with a rolling river behind her: Ayiiii, ayaaa, ayiiiayaaa, doesn't the neighbour's girl look beautiful today in the sunlight?

By the time the professor had reached the coffee-house and shushed all the men, Digin Hassig had begun humming a popular lovesong. The effect was not as great perhaps as a song of God, but when some of the men began softly to hum along the professor grew contented with his success, having proven to himself and to others the power of ideas made material.

The winter following the Virgin's nose wires, after deciding that Digin Hassig's chest cold was a maleficent and noise-making trouble and that he needed to see what was happening *inside* her chest cavity, the professor emerged with yet another idea made real after six days immersed in the Sinkhole.

This time when he quit the laboratory, rather than sitting down to a meal as he was wont to, he went in search of his wife. Digin Hassig sat in the salon with her embroidery on her lap and Mary at her feet reading verse by Varudjian. When Digin Hassig saw her unkempt and malodorous husband she stood abruptly, dropping her embroidery onto the open book. She asked, Husband, are you ready for dinner?

Voch voch, No no. Yegu, he commanded and, as if to emphasize his point, stuck out his index finger and called to his wife with it, like a headmaster intent on reprimanding a pupil. Digin Hassig followed him (unwillingly yet obediently, like a good wife) up the first and the second set of stairs. It was at the base of the second set that her heart began to pound in earnest. She had very seldom entered the laboratory and when she had, it had rarely been an occasion for amusement. Digin Hassig entered the Sinkhole after her husband and sat upon the English chair just as he ordered her to. She noticed the mounds of papery garlic clove shells covering the floor tiles. She wished she could stick both index fingers up her nose as her son Karnik had done the previous winter, but knowing she couldn't, she breathed through her mouth.

The professor aimed a strange apparatus at her chest and ordered her to tell him how she was feeling.

I'm fine, husband, she said, sucking air in through her teeth. My chest is fine now. See, she said and took a deep breath.

But you sound terrible, Hassig. Your nose is stuffed like a thick dolma. Sit still, eh-eh?

The professor then moved to the other side of the table and flipped a switch which made a light come on in the machine. Then he yelled out, *Ich kann sehen!* And his wife, alarmed by her husband's incomprehensible outburst, jumped up from the table and grabbed his arm and dug her nails into his skin, enquiring in a pitched voice, Eench-eh, eench-eh, eench-eh?

Well, my dear, he continued, I can tell you've a few rolls of fat and a strong stout heart.

To which Digin Hassig replied, Uf! and, beyond obedience and without patience, walked down to the second storey.

Despite the fact that Digin Hassig's condition had cleared up on its own prior to the professor's 'X-ray' photograph, he felt as if he'd triumphed once again. For weeks afterwards, the professor showed the picture of his wife's chest cavity to all interested parties and before long two other inquisitive men built their own X-ray machines using the professor's translation of the German treatise into Armenian. Soon pictures of hands and legs and a donkey's head circulated in the coffee-houses.

The professor concluded in his journals that although a chest cold is one of the most iniquitous maladies known to man, like anything evil it too eventually gets bored and moves on to newer pastures.

I Began with Sandals

I began the war with sandals on my feet as if it were July and August; a worn cotton shirt and later an overcape I requisitioned from a corpse. As a child I was told stories about the demons and the dev, but how could they have failed to mention that the inferno is an icy place? I begin with my toes, from ten there are now seven. I warm the frozen bazlama in the pit of my arms, and when it heats to body temperature, it crumbles in my fingers. I have ten fingers. When a scrap of meat appears in my hardened army cake, I whistle.

We are endless walkers for our nation. Piles of the men fall down on the mountain roads; mothers will not find their sons' black eyes twinkling over the rim of a hot cup of tea. I haven't tasted hot tea in more than a month. We have bazlama if we are lucky. Otherwise we forage on the plains and in the mountain forests; we requisition from the villagers.

The blizzard continues in all of its fury, and it is as if the earth is also our enemy. The snow and ice hit our faces like a whip master. We walk with our eyes closed in the wind. I'm not sure if *I* walk, but the body moves along of its own accord – the body makes the man move. I'm thinking of the wheat fields and a boy with a sickle in his hand. Of pilaf and tea and tea and hot soup. I'm thinking of shish kebab. Firuz died yesterday. He opened his mouth slightly and the man's thin bone arms stiffened as if made of wood or metal, his eyes frozen open in supplication. I wish he had had some shoes for me because today the strap broke on my left sandal and so one bare foot and one sandalled foot make the climb in the snow over the mountain. The Russian snow reaches our bellies sometimes and we do not speak as we walk. The country has become like a whore and yet I do not know what it would mean to go inside. What do the insides of buildings smell of?

My father was Kamil, and his father also; we are sons of the village of Tadim. I was in the field sowing the wheat when Firuz came to tell me of the call to arms. I did not wish to leave my home or my parents, but I understood that as Turkish men, this war was our duty, and on the appointed day Firuz and I walked the fifteen miles to the town of Mezre and waited to sign up. We waited for ten hours the first day. And then we waited for seven days more. We had only enough food for a few meals and so we were left to beg a piece of bread and onion from a kind passer-by or from one of the town boys waiting with us. The women regarded us with their pity. The effendi informed us that to leave Mezre would mean jail and execution. We sat in the courtyard with the hundreds and hundreds of other men and we sang beneath our breath and played backgammon with discarded pebbles.

116

One week later, we were sent back to our village and we were overjoyed. My father hugged his son and an-ne kissed my cheeks again and again. I was to be spared war. I was back in the fields and my wife, Sükran, brought me a special snack of honey and walnuts in the late afternoon. Two days later, the soldiers stopped by our home and informed my father I was a traitor and I was being arrested for not heeding the call to arms. We cried and pleaded and I left with them immediately. Baba gave me his sandals and the strongest shirt. I took three loaves of bread, and onions and some sheep's cheese. I left my sickle in the wheat field in the maddened rush.

I measure the snow for curiosity. Today it reaches my belly button, when last night it was at my knees! If you can break off a toe like a boiled sweet, don't put it in your mouth, Firuz advises me. Firuz was born two houses down from mine. He was six days older than me and because I had no older brothers he assumed the role. Don't forget your respectful bearing, he'd joke, and hold out his hand for a kiss. Firuz loved to show me the strength of his body; he used to bend his arms and proudly flash his round-hill muscles. When we planted the wheat fields he sang the bawdy songs: the girls with the golden hair, the golden hair, it's so golden everywhere. Firuz was the strongest man of Tadim and he was shoeless in Russia and his eyebrows connected in a black stiff line.

A few days ago, we passed a convoy of Russian prisoners. They wore thick cloaks on their backs and grey fur hats to protect their ears and faces – each man lifted his knee-high boots as if marching.

Salih, the company sergeant, tells the sick to walk to the hospital, six to eight days' distance from here.

It is certain death. We trudge on. Salih Effendi tells us we will have everything we need in the Russian villages. Chicken and tea, he says.

Today: Ali, Mehmet, Hamit, Arif, Fevzi died. Salih Effendi stands up and tells us again how the Armenians of Anatolia joined the battle with our age-old enemy and tried to strike our army in the back. The gâvurs' brethren live in Russia – would they fight against their own Armenian brothers? Did they fight with us in Yemen? Or in the Balkans? Didn't they buy our land for next to nothing while our corpses lay rotting in the desert? And so they became rich off of us; they have always been the money grubbers, merchant vultures. They stab us in our naked backs, they laugh at our chapped feet. We lost Greece, Bulgaria, and Serbia to the Christians. Will we lose again, brothers?

The Armenian regiment from Kharphert, the town boys, were taken off their duty and they hauled the carts. Then they were sent away from the lines, back to where they came from. We spit on their bent heads. Betrayers, we yelled, pelting them with roadside rock and debris. Dirty infidels.

Mustafa asks me if I can be his confidant and give his last words to his an-ne after the war. He has nothing to offer me; his shirt and trousers are in tatters. His feet have turned the ugly white from the bone-eating disease. Mustafa is a comedian. Recently he joked that the reason men went to war was to test the will and strength of their bowels. Before dying he confesses that he hasn't taken a shit in weeks. He begs me to advise his son, Timur, of his heroic feats.

We are the 36th division of the XI Corps. We captured the district of Oltu and continued on our way

118

to Bardiz. We began our march up the snow-covered jagged peaks of the Allah-I Ekber Mountains on 25 December. We marched for nineteen hours. Two of every three of us stayed behind in the cold snows of Russia.

Not I.

I sang the entire way, to warm the insides of my heart like a tonnir. I sang Firuz' favourite ditties for good measure. The bawdy songs.

When I was a boy an-ne used to warn me, Do not scratch behind your ears in anger, it will bring certain death. I hope I left a son in my wife's belly. The wheat fields are fallow in this winter cold and my implement for farming lies forgotten on the earth.

Official Proclamation

26 June 1915

Our Armenian fellow countrymen, who form one of the Ottoman racial elements, having taken up with a lot of false ideas of a nature to disturb the public order, as the result of foreign instigations for many years past, and because of the fact that they have brought about bloody happenings and have attempted to destroy the peace and security of the Ottoman state, of their fellow countrymen, as well as their own safety and interests, and, moreover, as the Armenian societies now have dared to join themselves to the enemy of their existence, and to the enemies now at war with our state, our Government is compelled to adopt extraordinary measures and sacrifices, both for the preservation of the order and security of the country, and for the continuation of their existence and for the welfare of the Armenian societies. Therefore, as a measure to be applied until the conclusion of the war, the Armenians have to be sent away to places which have been prepared in the interior vilayets, and a literal obedience to the following orders, in a categorical manner, is accordingly enjoined upon all Ottomans.

1. With the exception of the sick, all Armenians are obliged to leave, within five days from the date of this proclamation, and by villages or quarters, under the escort of the gendarmerie.

2. Although they are free to carry with them on their journey the articles of their movable property which they desire, they are forbidden to sell their landed and their extra effects, or to leave them here and there with other people. Because their exile is only temporary, their landed property, and the effects which they will be unable to take with them will be taken care of under the supervision of the Government, and stored in closed and protected buildings. Anyone who sells or attempts to take care of his movable effects or landed property in a manner contrary to this order shall be sent before the Court Martial. They are free to sell only to the Government, of their own accord, those articles which may answer the needs of the army.

3. To assure their comfort during the journey, hans and suitable buildings have been prepared, and everything has been done for their safe arrival at their places of temporary residence, without their being subjected to any kind of attack or affronts.

4. The guards will use their weapons against those who make any attempts to attack or affront the life, honour, and property of one or a number of Armenians, and such persons as are taken alive

will be sent to the Court Martial and executed. This measure being the regrettable result of the Armenians having been led into error, it does not concern in any way the other races, and these other elements will in no way or manner whatsoever intervene in this question.

5. Since the Armenians are obliged to submit to this decision of the Government, if some of them attempt to use arms against the soldiers or gendarmes, arms shall be employed only against those who use force, and they shall be captured dead or alive. In like manner, those who, in opposition to the Government's decision, refrain from leaving, or hide themselves here and there, if they are sheltered or are given food and assistance, the persons who thus shelter them or aid them shall be sent before the Court Martial for execution.

6. As the Armenians are not allowed to carry any firearms or cutting weapons, they shall deliver to the authorities every sort of arms, revolvers, daggers, bombs, etc., which they have concealed in their places of residence or elsewhere. A lot of such weapons and other things have been reported to the Government, and if their owners allow themselves to be misled, and the weapons are afterwards found by the Government, they will be under heavy responsibility and receive severe punishment.

7. The escorts of soldiers and gendarmes are required and are authorized to use their weapons against and to kill persons who shall try to attack or to

damage Armenians in villages, in city quarters, or on the roads for the purpose of robbery or other injury.

8. Those who owe money to the Ottoman Bank may deposit in its warehouse goods up to the amount of their indebtedness. Only in case the Government should have need thereof in the future are the military authorities authorized to buy the said goods by paying the price thereof. In the case of debts to other people it is permitted to leave goods in accordance with this condition, but the Government must ascertain the genuine character of the debt, and for this purpose the certified books of the merchant form the strongest proof.

9. Large and small animals which it is impossible to carry along shall be bought in the name of the army.

10. On the road the vilayet, leva, kaza and nahieh officials shall render possible assistance to the Armenians.

On Winter Evenings

ଗ୍ଞୋତ୍ରଓ

It was during the time when the oxen would wake us up each morning before sunrise as they pulled their heavy carts through town. The rik-rik of the ox carts awakened us and then lulled us back into warm blanketed sleep again and again. It was early spring when only the barest scent of the changing season was in the air; winter still stood like a white wall at our backs. The carters encouraged and goaded the new season on by decorating the oxen's unknotted horns with branches of white almond blossoms and their own caps with tiny pink bouquets of apple blossoms to distinguish themselves from their beasts. It was these adornments which made us think of hopefulness and soft grasses to tickle our unshod feet, of basketfuls of fruit picked directly from the orchard trees, of apples, apricot and fig popped into our waiting and remembering mouths.

Then it was unfettered blue freedom, bigger than the skies overhead. It roared in my ears like the river. I was a babe and my name was my own, the name Baba had christened me in 1901 before the Der Hyre in St Vartan's Church on the last day of the last month of spring after the rains had begun and before Baba would leave to travel and buy goods for the shop. Yes, I was born during the raining season, at the moment when the midwife said, Shud! and the flowers burst their buds.

My birth, I want you to know, my darling, was in the clear morning. Mama sat upon the birthing stool and midwife Siroun was saying, Goodgirl, goodgirl, push this miracle of God to light, give this babe this light. Perhaps one day the child will be your strength, Yughaper.

So Mama pushed and because I was an obedient girl when Siroun told me to come I arrived at the beginning of April. Life was sweet at Mama's breast, you remember. Mairig's heartbeat reminded me of the world I'd somewhat reluctantly left behind. Eventually I realized I was here to stay and therefore had best begin adjusting and start living in the here and now. I ate a few bites of mashed wheat gruel and I was, alas, set free from Mama.

One night Mama took me up onto the flat roof while Baba slept. The moon was full and large like an opal, opalescent. The moon hung above the distant peaks of Mount Ararat. Father Moon, Mama said, holding me up, this is the girl who holds my heart.

I looked at the opalescent moon, my body wrapped tightly in Mama's shawl, and the moon called to me loudly in the springtime silence, which was the silence of pink and white blossoms and the lowing cows and the Arab mare next to our house neighing into the night; the moon whispered in my heart.

I became the girl with the too-thick nose and the

long brown plaits that tickled the backs of her knees when she walked; the girl who helped her baba in the garden with the sweet watermelon and the green okra; the girl who schooled and learned to read. Mama bore three boys after me and then many years later you came to us, our blue-eyed rose: Nevart. This is what you must remember, this we must never forget, the moon whispered to me that night: that blood is the thickest, the tightest dark coil.

Nene Heripsime gathered the washed and carded wool with the neighbourhood ladies and they spun it into beautiful white cocoons around their fists and arms and flattened hands. Mairig would take me with her to Nene's house when I was a small girl. She helped the aunties with their work; I sat on a cushion in the corner and watched the house become like a snowy season inside as well as out. I waited for the woollen butterflies to burst from their winter homes.

The aunties would sing as they worked, as they later sewed and knitted clothes for the cold season. In the afternoon they would break and take tea, the fruit tray would pass around the circle and each woman would pick up a dried apple or apricot or fig and taste the season when the fruit was on the bough. Those were the days when the doors were never locked, when a stranger could come to your home and stay for one day or one month and receive your hospitality like proffered fruit, like a lighted wax candle.

Twenty-seven, twenty-eight, twenty-nine. Anaguil counts for her blue-eyed sister, teaching her her numbers; she holds the little girl's fingers up and then presses them down again. Thirty! Nevart yells out. Her pink fingers lie against her palms and the blue-eyed girl laughs. Nevart holds up her two closed fists. Thirty-one, thirty-two, thirty-three, she continues, her fingers lifting up with the one and the two and the three.

Anaguil listens to Nevart counting, and she remembers how she used to listen to the rhyming games her mother played with her and her brothers. She recalls the years before the age of eight when she wasn't expected always to act like a young lady. When she hadn't been required to watch her tongue and tuck her legs beneath her tightly and kneel in church for hours without giggling. When she could still play games with Rachel and Haigan; when she could run in the garden and muddy her clothes and throw ripened pomegranates at the boys from her quarter. When a girl dies, the ground must approve; while she lives, the public must approve, Nene Heripsime used to scold her.

Anaguil remembers how hard it was to lose freedoms. Every year as she got older more things were taken away, until finally eleven descended with her menses and she could never again climb the trees and make ugly faces at her brothers. Her brothers played on without her: in the garden, in their bedroom, in the attic and in the cellar. Boys' games for boys only. Anaguil learned to embroider, and to spin wool in the winter, to make baklava, and to bring her baba his slippers and empty his ashtrays. She began the work to fill her hope chest for her wedding day. All of these things I would love now, she thinks. I would not complain when Mama required me to do my stitches anew.

Fatma! Do you hear?

Anaguil lifts her eyes to blue-eyed Nevart and cuffs

her on the head. Never call me that privately. Call me nothing, if you cannot remember. But never call me that.

And both girls cry.

Eh, little girl, your sister will tell you a story, Anaguil whispers in Nevart's ear late in the evening when the household is quiet and the two sisters are hunched underneath the multicoloured woollen blankets.

Mairig was an angel from the heavens who lit up the house like a thousand lighted candles burning before the image of Mother Mary. She kissed Hayrig each day and brought him his slippers and made a rice pilaf whose rich butter flavour floated through the chimney smoke and out into the town air, bringing neighbours from miles around begging for a portion. Please Sister Yughaper, may we try a bite of your delicious golden pilaf? the townswomen would say, wanting to, in their small tastes, taste the difference and discover the magic of Mama's pilaf. Mairig had a secret, Anaguil whispers, and she whispers in the forbidden language like she has every evening for the past one year and nine months. She drops these fragments into Nevart's pink and folded ear. Anaguil understands that the stories she tells her sister make her *her* sister and not some other girl: a Mohammedan girl, a dilek for their Allah, Dilek who has forgotten the Lord. As the Lord has forgotten us, the idea will sometimes crowd into Anaguil's mind.

Anaguil, eench *secret*? What does this mean, what does that mean? Nevart wonders in her broken Armenian and Anaguil translates into the Turkish. Life, she says. A secret is life.

Poetry

It has been seventeen weeks, three days, five hours and a certain amount of minutes and seconds and measures smaller than seconds – diminutive time capsules like fly eggs, thousands of spotted and uncountable time-eggs – since I've lived here in this attic where the heat melts the hairs off my arms, and the constant perspiration on my skin has brought on a mutiny of red-pus sores. I am like a hairless dog, like the bitches who live behind the hamam, who burn to nothing and who die but still go again and again to the hamam in search of comfort. I used to see them in the winter in the alleyway behind the bathhouse, cuddling in the ashes the hotwater attendants would dump in a heap outside the back door of the baths: the same dogs reincarnated over and over again. The people living there among the embers would kick the mongrels and cook them when all of their fur had been singed and removed, when their raised sanguine sores had made patterns on their skin – a facsimile of a new coat. It was an outdoor barbecue, reminiscent of summertime feasts.

Who shall cook me?

You, Turkish reed-sharpener, will you eat a dog although of another (and now repellent) race?

My death will be like a dog's, like a hamam-dog's dying days in the heat of the ashes. I've removed my woman's vestments; I am the new Adam in the garden, the Garden of Heat-in-the-Attic: Sargis, the modern vitreous poet. I'll tell You of my dark days in this oven. I'm cooking. You'll eat me unseasoned in strips with bread. (Will you have bread then for your sandwich? Will the bakeries re-open?)

Poem 1

Soothe! Soothe! Soothe!
Like spring bushes, Soothe!
Not the colour of lilacs or the green spike leaves or the
    wide-flung ocean,
And again another, rigid and hard,
But your love soothes not me, not me.

Your mother rose late,
Like the low-hanging moon – O I think this vessel is
    heavy with love's suffering.

I call to you, touch you.
See, see, see,
See how I love.

We are forever apart,
We can be together no longer.
O past! O sunned death!
Loved! Loved! Loved!

Are you losing your mind, Sargis? Mama whispers, wishing she could yell in the late-afternoon swelter as she climbs the ladder to bring me my afternoon meal. Sargis, hokees, put some clothes on. Darling, what are you doing? she asks as I continue my writing hunched over the stool, reed-pen in hand, small book of poems spread open across my knees. My arsehole itches. The sores on my forearms touch the yellow paper, leaving round stains like bloomed poppies.

I don't look at Mairig. I've cleaned my fingers. I rub them together. (Does she think a little shit-staring will make me crazy? I'm preparing. Mama, do you know what it means to get ready?)

I keep daily records of my excrement. Its changes. Its abeyances. Its textures: adamantine, fleshy, bushy, lithe, gelatinous, flaccid. What would its utterances be? I write my caca poems.

For three days now there is nothing, only urine urine urine: yellow, gold, puce, quince, buff, sea-sand (O, lovely!), desert-sand. I strain. I think: I am dying. My arsehole hurts, the wrinkled squeeze-hole is like another burn. I sit on a cushion. My mama's needle-work massages my bare arse – cream flowers and round edges caress me.

I long for the gendarmes to come again. Yes. I long for their marching. Their orders. Out. Shut up. Fucking Armenian cur. When they come at night I sit on my bowl and the universe (more than just the town) flows out of me like soup, like sweet-come, like fir tree sap, like a corner drinking fountain, like Love – God's Love, Holy Water – and I am Free and I am Lightness. Body of Christ. Body of my Body. My own words. What else is there?

My greatest desire is to shit in a liquid stream and

to come at the same time. I masturbate as I squat over the enamel basin with the blue chip. Like an ancient god. I wait for the police to arrive; I hold my cock in my hands. I wait for You. Time slows as I sit on my bowl and I look up at the small window in the corner of the attic. I can make out a few stars, and I count the fly eggs, one at a time.

Beneath the dome of the white summer sky the books burned as if without remorse. The Holy Bibles, the history and exegesis, the poetry and the algorithms and lists of pharmaceutical items, the epic poems and seventeenth-century dictionaries were licked up by the blue and yellow pyre, like darting pubescent tongues sucking on a sweet ice. The handwritten books, the books with gold-etched drawings, the books that had carefully been concealed and guarded for hundreds of years burned like any stick of wood or scrap of cigarette paper or piece of littered dung. They were unnostalgic fires, lacking a reverence for history and a Christian God; in general they lacked respect for the written word. Thus it was that the hand-written Gospel from the fourteenth century, painstakingly copied onto sheepskin and still in its original Gerabar, which only the scholars read today, was devoured indiscriminately with the imported modern books from Constantinople detailing the newest discoveries in locomotion.

The gendarmes piled the books of the Armenian quarter, in the language that they and the massed crowd could not speak, high into the night. Some books were kept apart and taken to the barracks: they were chosen for the quality of their paper, and stacked haphazardly in the kitchens. Cooks wiped out the soup bowls with excerpts of fourteenth-century lyric poems and the epic of Sassoun.

Was my training for this? How could I have known that it would all come down to this room? This darkness? These sad days of lost hope? Did I miss the signs? Did you give us any signs, Lord?

The History of Bozmashen as Iterated by the Local Dogs

☙❧

A shepherd boy took his flock miles from home in the summer months. He searched with his dogs and his sheep on the high plateau for sweet grasses. The days passed and the boy did not see another person from his village or even a local Kurd or Turk pedlar. He travelled from stream to stream where he filled his leather drinking bag.

Isquhee the shepherd boy conversed with his dogs over dinner. The black and brown bitch, and the white spotted mongrel, whose back legs gave out after hours of walking, listened attentively.

This year I'll marry. She'll have to be a goodgirl, modest. Industrious. You won't be jealous, will you?

Not in the least.

Her pilaf must be excellent as well. Extrabuttery.

Of course.

And her breath must be extrasweety.

. . .

Not too hairy either.

Isquhee ate the remainder of his soukhari.

The following evening Isquhee sat around the small fire with his two dogs listening to the sheep baaing into the night.

She'll have to be beautiful. Her breasts full. Her thighs should touch to the knee. You won't mind sleeping beneath the bed in winter, will you? She may not like two dogs' company on the blankets.

Not in the least.

You can keep each other warm.

Yes.

And of course we'll be busy in wintertime.

. . .

The shepherd boy returned to his village in the morning. The wind was quiet in the eaves and trees and down the narrow dirt roads of his district. His mother saw him when he eased the front door open; she jumped up from her chair by the hearth and grabbed him.

Son, you've come home early. Is there something amiss?

No, no, Mairig, nothing except a persistent itch on the nape of my neck. And the howling of the dogs began to bother me so much I couldn't eat or sleep. They didn't howl into the night as they've always done, but rather from the middle of my very ears. They climbed inside my ears, Mairig.

Inside of them, son?

Yes, the howls were like the Euphrates. They were unstoppable, relentless. I am ashamed to say this constant howling, keening like a nightmare ghost, made me cry.

Tell me, Isquhee, what stories have you been telling?

Isquhee put his water carrier and his duduk on the floor by the hearth and he sat at his mother's knees.

I began to think of my future wife. Her – pardon me, Mairig – breasts and thighs.

Did you mention her lips or her forehead?

No, I wasn't concerned with those.

Her buttocks? Bend at the knee? Second toes which are longer than the big toe? Chin wrinkle?

No and no and no, Mairig.

Did you imagine her knuckle lines? The hairs growing from her nipples? Her dry and flaky elbow skin?

Voch.

Did you realize that she will stink and vomit? Pimples will form on her arse. She will shit in piles.

. . .

How are your ears now, my son?

. . .

Close your eyes and rest awhile. Tomorrow you will feel better.

In the morning Mairig rose at dawn and emptied the nightpan filled with urine. She stirred the fire and boiled the water for tea. Isquhee still slept in front of the hearth. The black and brown bitch, and the white spotted mongrel, whose back legs gave out after hours of walking, curled around him. They snored.

Breakfast time, my babies! Mairig yelled.

All three dogs awoke at the sound *breakfasttimemybabies* and jumped up wagging their tails.

I had a terrible dream last night, *mybabies*. The world as we know it came to a crossroads. And afterwards there was no kifteh or pots of yogurt soup the way you like them in this land. There was no one to light the tonnir. A real nightmare.

At eight o'clock Kurken the shepherd boy came to gather the dogs and prepare the flock for the summer months on the high plateau looking for sweet grasses.

Have a good time, my nephew. Be careful up there. The stories circulate like a gnats' black cloud and can mislead a man.

Kurken looked at his auntie strangely. All three dogs followed him when he whistled and left the small mudbrick house. When Kurken reached the first stream outside of the village he began to feel faint. His thoughts returned to his auntie's words. He decided he needed more soukhari for the summer and he turned around and headed back to his auntie's house to secure some.

When he covered the approximate distance he had just travelled, he found only a few large white stones in the place where the village should have been. The earth was parched. The field mice ran around freely and the three dogs chased them with hungry glee.

This is strange. I don't find the village.

He continued walking, thinking perhaps that he had taken a wrong turn, although as a son of the village he could not imagine a wrong turn from the first spring. He walked until he came upon a sole policeman dressed as a poor farmer in the middle of a fallow wheat field. The Turkish or Kurdish farmer, who was or was not a policeman, held a sickle in his hand and with thrashing movements cut at the weeds growing there.

Effendi, I'm lost. Can you tell me how to get to Bozmashen?

Bozma-heh? Bozma-heh? Why, I'll kill you, you whore's son!

And with that he ran towards Kurken with his farming implement raised.

Sir, how have I offended you?

Bozma-heh! Bozma-heh!

The policeman in farmer's clothing swiped Kurken's head cleanly off.

Isquhee and the black and brown bitch, and the white spotted mongrel, whose back legs gave out after hours of walking, licked at the fountain of the boy's blood rushing from his neck.

And three apples fell from heaven: one for the storyteller, one for the listener, and one for the eavesdropper.

American Consulate
Mamouret-ul-Aziz (Harput), Turkey
December 30, 1915

Honorable Henry Morgenthau,
American Ambassador,
Constantinople

Sir:

I have the honor to continue my reports of June 30, July 11, July 24, August 23 and September 7 (File No. 840.1) about the deportation and massacre of the Armenians in this region, as follows:

The last four months have been full of uncertainty and anxiety for everyone. There has been no security for any of the few Armenians who were left here after the deportation of July and August, and no assurance worth listening to that the Armenian question is ended. The town crier has announced once or twice by order of the Vali that no more Armenians would be sent away and that all could come out without fear, but the falsity of such announcements was shown a few weeks later by the wholesale arrest and deportation of those who had ventured out in reliance upon them. The ruse worked so well that it will probably be repeated and, no matter how many times this may occur, I have no doubt that others will be caught in the same way as long as any remain. There seems to be as much reason to apprehend a further arrest and deportation now of the few Armenians who remain here as there has been at any time during the last six months. No one knows whether the few who have escaped thus far will be spared in the end or whether those who are perpetrating this crime, the most awful, probably, that has ever been committed against any race of people, will continue until the last Armenian in the country has been killed.

The predictions made and fears expressed in my early reports upon this subject have been for the most part all too fully realized. As two of them (Nos 62 of June 30 and 71 of July 24) were apparently lost in the mails or intercepted by the authorities, I am sending copies of these reports in accompanying despatch No. 172 of yesterday. It will be noticed that they are not reports that were intended to be read by Turkish officials, but I presume that is what happened to them. The receipt of my reports of July 11, August 23 and September 7 has been acknowledged.

One of the most remarkable incidents in the terrible tragedy that is being enacted has been the sale by the Government at public auction of great quantities of second-hand clothing that had been taken from the backs of the deported Armenians who were killed. Many bundles of such clothing were brought in town and the sale continued in the marketplace for many days. I am told that the same thing took place in the other towns of this vilayet. I saw it going on here myself. One can hardly imagine anything so sordid or gruesome. Another act of barbarism still more frightful, which has been related to me by survivors of the massacres, is that the gendarmes sold them in groups of fifty or a hundred to the Kurds, who were to kill them and could have whatever they could find on them. As most of the persons deported were thoroughly searched and robbed by the gendarmes the Kurds seldom obtained more than a few old clothes from the persons whom they killed. Thus the so-called 'deportation' of the Armenians has been carried on!

The term of 'Slaughterhouse Vilayet' which I applied to this vilayet in my last report upon this subject (that of September 7) has been fully justified by what I have learned and actually seen since that time. It appears that all those in the parties mentioned on page 15 of that report, men, women and children, were massacred about five hours distant from here. In fact, it is almost certain that, with the exception of a very small number of those who were deported during the first few days of July, all who have left here have been massacred before reaching the borders of the vilayet. It is somewhat difficult to understand the plan by which people were brought all the way here from Trebizond, Urdu, Kherassou, Zara, Erzurum and Erzincan, only to be butchered in this vilayet. During the last two months quite a number of Armenian soldiers have been brought back in groups of two or three hundred from Erzurum. They have arrived in a most pitiable state due to their exposure on the way at this season of the year and the privations they had suffered. After all they had endured and after having been brought this far it appears that nearly all of them were killed a few hours after leaving here. A few have escaped and have related how the gendarmes tied them together a short distance out of town. Their dead bodies may be seen all alongside of the road. The rest of them are said to have been taken a little further and killed in the mountains. One of the sad sights of this town now is to see companies of these soldiers being brought here every little while when we know that they are to be butchered like animals. We are all wondering why this vilayet is chosen as the slaughterhouse.

Of nearly a hundred thousand Armenians who were in this vilayet a year ago, there are probably not more than four thousand left. It has been reported recently that no more than five percent of the Armenians were to be left. It is doubtful if that many remain now. There are probably more in proportion in the two towns of Mamouret-ul-Aziz and Harput than elsewhere because many have come from the villages in which no Armenians now remain or can live and have sought shelter here. It is estimated that between one-third and one and one-half of the entire existing Armenian population of this vilayet is now in these two towns and in two or three of the neighboring villages, but the persons above mentioned who have recently come here form a considerable portion of this number.

In my brief despatch No. 170 of yesterday I spoke of the pressure that is being brought on nearly all the Armenian women here, including wives of naturalized Ottomans, to embrace the Muslim faith. As directed in Embassy's Instruction of November 30, I endeavor to dissuade them from taking this step. A very large number of women have come to me about this matter during the last few weeks. They say they are threatened with deportation, which means almost certain death, if they refuse. It is by no means improbable that this will actually be the result of such a refusal in many cases. I shall do everything possible, of course, to save from either fate all women who are in any way entitled to American protection.

One of the disappointments in the present terrible situation and one of the saddest commentaries on American missionary work among the Armenians is their lack of religious and moral principles and the general baseness of the race. During all that has happened during the past year I have not heard of a single act of heroism or of self-sacrifice and the noble acts, if any, have been very few. On the contrary mothers have given their daughters to the lowest and vilest Turks to save their own lives; to change their religion is a matter of little importance to most of the people; lying and trickery and an inordinate love of money are besetting sins of almost all, even while they stand in the very shadow of death. Absolute truthfulness is almost unknown among the members of this race. Money is sought at any price, even at the risk of their lives. Every trick and device are resorted to by those who are not in need as well as by those who are in much greater need. From every point of view the race is one that cannot be admired, although it is one to be pitied.

The present is the time to consider its needs and not its merits. The thousand or two Armenians in this immediate vicinity are for the most part entirely destitute and dependent upon charity. Practically all who remain here are women and children and few of them have the means with which to buy bread or any way of earning it. I shall be very glad to assist in such work as far as I can, as I have been doing with the funds already sent by the Embassy for that purpose and shall do with such additional funds as the Embassy may be able to send.

The important thing is to keep people alive for the present and then to assist them to leave the country as soon as it may be possible. There is no way of knowing, however, what further measures may be taken against the few survivors who remain here and the difficulty under present conditions of saving any in case of emergency from the cutthroats of this region is perhaps the greater than can be easily realized by those who are living in more civilized places. The only effective way I have found, as I previously explained, has been to keep people in the Consulate itself and naturally the number who can be saved in that way is limited.

I have the honor to be, sir,
Your obedient servant,
    Leslie Davis, Consul

[In cipher.]
I intend to supplement these reports on the deportation and massacre of the Armenians with an account of two trips which I made to a lake about 5 hours distant from here where I saw the dead bodies of fully 10 thousand persons, many of whom had recently been killed, and to illustrate it with photographs which I took of them alive in camps. It would not be prudent to send such a report now.

Davis looks up from his desk, he lifts the seal and presses it into the thick sheaf of papers. He hears the town crier in the distance.

Garabed! he yells from his desk.

The cavass runs into his office.

What is that boy yelling on the streets now?

Sale

❧❧❧

We have been given nine days. Nine days with which to bargain and sell and give away or throw out, safeguard an item or more of our lifetime possessions; to abnegate our property and ourselves. We have been told it is illegal to sell and they have been told it is prohibited to buy, but the gendarmes do not intervene and the marketplace ensues.

Everyone is outside for the first time in weeks, the women and the old men who remain – desiccated souls, down-turned visages. The sun is high and warms our neck and shoulders. We do not smile into the wind as we once did; you will not see our men dancing the circle dance with their arms raised together to form a parapet. Who sings? Mama taught me to be frugal and I do not know what it means to *throw away*. Like the other ladies and children in the gutter today selling our households, I do not know what it means to make sense of this perfidy.

I sit on the street and I sell and barter and I argue with the Turkish women to give them our sewing machine, the rugs, the pots, the wooden carved chair, the pillows and coverlets. Not that! Nishan screamed as I piled on Baba's suits, but today I am cold I am bitter, manifold – I can do anything.

Take it, whore-daughters. The orphan girl will give it all to you. Is that her haggling with the fruit-seller's wife over the price of soup bowls? Give it away like spit. Take it with you, take it with you! Is that her accepting fifty paras for the copper trays and the por-celain plates Hagop brought from Europe? The baleful bitches do not offer a fair price in the Armenian quar-ter marketplace. They know that it all must go. They are remorseless women like beetles in a cave. Even the rich women have come to the quarter today seeking a good bargain. Where is the pity of it?

Four days. Take it with you, take us for less; the strap from the plough beam is no longer harnessed to the yoke – these inchoate days unmake the farmer's dying wish. The woollen blankets and silken shawls. The backgammon board and the embroidery needles. Our mule was taken. I wonder if they'll also take Hanik, our nightingale. He sits in his cage and he does not sing.

Mama: may I sell your dresses?

Baba, I gave your shoes to the Turkish pot-fixer. He had none. He took them and did not offer thanks; he placed them on his head and dragged off the neigh-bour's saddle. The police chief's wife went to Madame Minassian's door three days ago with an escort of gen-darmes. She said, I'll care for the organ while you're away, and the men went in and pulled out the shiny brown organ and loaded it onto the waiting cart. She took three of their large rugs also. I'll keep them safe, the rich lady said, and moved her men and the cart down the street to the next row of houses.

Mama, what can she keep? What will give her a little piece of Mama and Baba for as long as she can keep it? She thinks about the boys. They are upstairs in the attic. She will not let them come out onto the crowded streets, the stolid quarter has become the marketplace – everything is for sale and the desiccated souls. She senses the keen joy in the buyers – a bargain is the most erotic prospect. It pushes the blood into the cheeks and down to the groin. A seller who must sell, who cannot set her own prices. It is better than free; they are slatterns for the hungry.

They have us already, Mama, in the palms of their hands and between their shoving legs. They tell us we will be safe on the journey to the Der-el-Zor, but we know, Mama, we know that they have us already.

Stepan is upstairs hiding, our youngest and heartful boy. His seven years make it more difficult for him to understand, but they have taken too many of them, and I will not allow him to come outside. Nishan and Jirair are silent watchers in the attic; it is only Nevart who cries. She sits next to me in the gutter, she cries for you and your flowered dress and your sweet milk. I would cry also, but all of my tears have been sold. There are no hidden springs in Anaguil. Obdurate girl, they say to me.

I release Hanik today, Baba. Our together nightingale. He left us also. Alone here in this high and unreachable house. The house I have known all of my life. How can I bargain him also?

Hanik? Hanik? I sing to him. Come back to us, my dear. Did you only stay because of your cage? Hanik. Hokees Hanik. Go tell Baba. Tell him when you see him that I am keeping his Waltham pocket watch. I will wear it later. When it is safe to wear jewellery and it is blue skies and blue silk days for the unabashed.

Gülhan Hanim came to us today. She kissed me and I could have fallen. She squeezed my hands and held Nevart to her breast. She says she will aid us, Mama. Murat Agha was called into the army three days ago. He is also gone, departed for the Russian mountains or for the Dardanelles. Murat Agha said to her on his last night, We will care for Hagop Demirdjian's children, I gave my partner my inviolate word. Gülhan Hanim has told me: she keeps this promise to Baba. She kissed me and I could have fallen. I understand the risk she takes for herself and her family in giving us this aid.

And so Mama. And so. We are going to Gülhan Hanim's house. She lives with her mother-in-law – there are no men in the house now except for her boy, Ahmet, and Baby Bülent and the old servant, Ismet. She will send the boys to the Turkish village of Tadim where they have a farm. They will be safer there, Mama, where the gendarmes and soldiers are not always walking the streets and searching the houses. Nevart and I will stay with Gülhan Hanim in town. This town. Our Kharphert.

I'm giving it all away, Mama. What will be left? This house we'll leave tomorrow before the gendarmes come for us to send us away. We have told no one that we are leaving, not even Madame Minassian next door. She cries all of the time, Mama, your old friend

Madame Minassian, the beautiful lady with the five boys she was so proud of. She sits alone in her empty house; there are square shadows on the floor where the rugs once lay. I remember how she used to say she was blessed with all boys and no girls to build a dowry for. Now she is a solitary bead, Mama. She has pulled her hair out like so many ladies. She moans and prays to God to take her life also. The gendarmes in the street laugh at her prayers.

Madame Minassian is all alone, Mama; she is a solitary bead. I went next door yesterday to take her some food. But she will not eat. Anaguil, she said, I am hastening death. Help me ease from this life. They have taken the light from my eyes; my breast is a tomb. What else is there?

But there is always more, Mama, to be taken. Today the soldiers went in through her front door. A pretty lady alone. Today there is no Madame Minassian and tomorrow we will go with Gülhan Hanim. The boys will wear my hemmed dresses. The servant, Ismet, will come to get us. With all of the frenzy in the streets I hope that we will not be noticed. I cannot take much, Mama. Only what I can carry in unnoticeable bundles. I am deciding. I am in charge. Nishan helps me make decisions. He says to keep only the gold and jewellery.

(I have been sleeping in your bed, Mama. I smell you in the linen and each morning I loathe to rise.)

I am keeping your headscarf. I will guard your bath sandals. Your yellow church dress. I will tuck the family photograph that we took before blue-eyed Nevart joined us into my pocket. I keep these things that touched your skin.

(Lying in your bed it is as if you are still here.)

*   *   *

148

I am baking bread. I am baking some of the gold coins into bread. Golden loaves. I'll make a payment to Gül- han Hanim to keep us, as Baba instructed you and you instructed me. I've unearthed the gold, Mama, and I am baking bread. I'll make weekly payments to Gülhan Hanim and she'll hide us. Until when? Mama. Mama. I have no tears left in me. When you left us eight days ago they departed also. You are keeping them in your hidden breast pocket.

Mama, we'll become her children. We'll be their Turkish boys and girls. I've got to use a new name, Gülhan Hanim told me. Mama, this summer we all will have new names.

Inside, 1917

There is always the interrogative. The why. Why? –
this house or that house closer to the centre of town?
– did Rachel unplait her hair before she cut it off,
before she left it outside the well; before she later
dropped her self inside the dark place? – does she recall
dried pink figs and not pilaf or kifteh as their last meal
together? – couldn't she find Mama's gold-drop ear-
rings in time to keep them? – is she tired from the
moment she wakes until the moment she lays herself
down next to Nevart to sleep and only then does she
feel a wakefulness like a chilled hand? – did she never
notice her hands before; the detail and etched filigree
on the tips of each finger, like fine jewellery, like gold-
smith's pride? – does Nevart play so much with other
children, as if she has always known them, as if they
can be her friends; does Nevart hold Gülhan Hanim's
hand so tightly, like a daughter, so frequently? – more
than all else does she crave the indoors now, seated
or standing in front of a square-glass window framing
the outdoor landscape; does she love the world in bits
and pieces through glass; does every bit of window-

glass make her turn her head to stare outside; does she love the inside now but only when she can see (a little bit) to the outside? – have one year and nine months passed and still there is no end to the fighting and the hiding? – the aching in her protruding chest bones like a rough lattice work on the body? – are her breasts already so much larger than she remembers Mama's were? – Baba? – Mama? (– *me*?)

Estivation

❧

If I were the wolf in winter I would seek such a cave and bury my body there for the cold season. Myself and my sucklings wrapped in circular comfort by the body. Held tightly in my arms; the bright summer is the evil quarter.

This summer 1915 has made the town a carnival. Incarnate. Why is it no one steps from the line, no one will kill them? One of them. We, and I, wait quietly with our savage moans to God who does not listen. We beg for water and for the hardest black loaves. We have already offered the prettiest girl to gendarme, soldier, Kaimakam. We do not stand, but bow low.

We would be snails who crawl inside ourselves in the summertime. Estivating beasts. I envy the smallest insects, the black fly who glances my shoulder and tips off toward the sky. The locust swarms, killers and cloud catchers. The louse who brings the sickness in small bites.

I will write a letter to Elia. I have never written to him before and honestly with my truth between my fingers, I cannot recall his face. He was never the man I loved. No. It was arranged as all marriages should be. Elia, the drug-store pharmacist. A slim man, bespectacled. And Lucine, Setrak the dentist's daughter. An educated girl, gifted embroiderer and lover of history lessons.

One afternoon after we were married we went to my parents' home for Sunday dinner. I remember we ate the most delicious kebabs and the bread rose in piles from the table. I ate very little that day, I cannot recall why. I could not finish my portion of lamb and my mother complained or I gave it to my husband. I think of that filled plate and I long to have it back, like a removed hand desires its lost shadow. I can remember exactly the outlines of kebab and onion and tomato, better than my husband's cheek and tongue. Do you see how strange this world has become?

Elia was an industrious man and a kinder husband. He was hardly filled with harsh words but with gentle touches and even a bearer of small hidden gifts. His mother, my zocanch, was 'better than some and not as bad as others'. I kissed her hand dutifully and I listened when she spoke. I rinsed the soap and clay from her back at the hamam. I miss the old lady here. And the rules of meal times, and even the locked larder. I don't think of the others. I don't think of the others.

Elia is digging trenches. Or Elia is hauling dung. He used to wear his European clothes with pride, his cravat and three-button suit jacket. He was a slim man, a man who now hauls dung or digs trenches. He was never the man I loved, but now he could be such a man. His hands were kind, they signed *Paid in Full* beautifully, like a rosette. I will not write him this letter. This history lesson filled only with speakable things.

The Seljuk Turks conquered Constantinople in the fifteenth century. And for many years afterwards, we were their *millet i-sadika*, their loyal community: obedient, industrious. In 1908 we celebrated together and Turk kissed Armenian and Armenian shook his hand with his Hope. We didn't think about the Sassun massacres of 1894 or of Adana; we shook his hand with Hope. In 1908 it was our new constitution, and it was equality for all the millets. My father, the dentist, the Euphrates College man, celebrated wildly with his hands in the air. We will be free to choose, he said. And you, Lucine, will read our history in many languages.

You are not surprised that Setrak the dentist put gold in people's mouths. Or that Setrak the dentist was pulled from his bed at night, protesting wildly with his hands in the air. Hopeful hands. They removed them in front of my mother. Returned his hands. Still twinkling. They tied his arms together, but not tightly enough at first, and the rope slipped loose down the arm-stems and fell to the ground. There were two dentist hands on the floor of our home. They lay perched like turtles in the lake of blood (or perhaps they were caves, snail shells). The nails were clean and cut into the shape of squares.

On the morning of 5 July the people of our quarter waited for the police to come and direct them on the road to Mesopotamia. We huddled together in the salon, lined up in rows: Zocanch, Elia's youngest sister, the maiden aunt, the sisters-in-law, the two or three girl cousins: fifteen or twenty of us, and me also; my zocanch held her youngest granddaughter in her arms. Each of us had a bundle to carry: beans or bulgur or water. The smallest children wore gold tucked into their sleeves and hair; all of us had sewn invisible pockets into the hems of our old and tattered dresses where we carried our jewellery and gold pieces. We waited to leave in the early morning. We looked like beggar women. We had cut our hair; rubbed ash into our cheeks. We had heard the rumours about exile, and we knew and we lined up in rows in the salon of our home. We left our shorn hair in the corners of the house.

It was not yet hot that morning. I held my son's hand and waited for the gendarmes to come to our home. I held my son's hand, my boy dressed in his girl cousin's clothing. Through the window I heard an ancient oxen let out its heavy breath or the mourning doves were sending messages to one another from the orchard boughs. I stood up in the salon and I turned towards the back door. I sat again. I said I would return immediately and I stood and pulled my boy up and I left the bundle of bulgur on the floor. Voch, my zocanch said.

With the boy I walked to the edge of town and found the hidden path down to Mezre. We ran together. My son asked, Lucine? – because he had learned in our private lessons – Lucine, ur gertank? Where are we going?

I do not think of later. Or of our weak song: who sings at their own killing? My father raised his arms when they asked him to, so that the cleft would be flawless. Skin then bone then two turtles or caves or snail shells. I know of the thousand at the cemetery. They were deported from Garin and Dikranagerd and Erzincan.

It is hot in Kharphert in the summertime and the cemetery is filled with cypresses and their shadows. They have walked and they will walk further. Get up, the police say to them, and they lift themselves up and they leave behind one hundred or two hundred and also small children. The ox carts come in the evening. The bodies are thrown onto the carts one at a time. The corpse-handlers complain about the terrible stench and the immodesty of the naked women; they throw lye onto the bodies to make sure everyone is dead. There is talk here that the men in the army have dug their own burial trenches. Elia is hauling dung.

My son and I made a path to Mezre. Perhaps I am the first woman in our history to walk unchaperoned in the three-mile wilderness. Of her own volition.

Some Turks have always spit in our faces. They have called us gâvur. Infidel. Inferior. I found the path at the steepest incline and walked down the hill to Mezre. I walked to Ambar Mahallesi Street. In my school English I said, My father in America. We American. And I was allowed inside the tall gate.

My zocanch and the others were not deported immediately. The mark of Cain on their door faded in the weeks it took the gendarmes to organize their quarter's departure. I can see them still, the young and old ladies, our children, lined up in rows, waiting.

You, You Also Break Me

I remember the hamam clearly from my childhood. Mairig dragged me and my siblings to the baths twice a month. We washed and excreted, we were ardent; I spit in the little pools and in the corners. As children we poked and prodded. Melkon was the pharmacist and I was his patient; Koharig rubbed me softly when I was ill. We touched and played and in the distance the water poured from the faucets and the women unravelled their hair and lifted their distended breasts. They arranged marriages and appraised the young girls. We saw their big thighs and double knees. Their fatty arses and hairy pubes. We children looked from our corners, we looked at the women and then we looked at our smooth forms. We preferred our smoothness.

I was terrified of the women and their hairy groins. I felt pity for Koharig, who would become one of them. I hoped she would be a girl for ever, or perhaps become a man, who I assumed did not suffer such abomination.

Once I left behind the world of women, I never returned.

On the evening the hamam was reserved for men I went with Hayrig. I was seven or eight years old.

(What should I fear now? You shall devour me. I will become the beloved. The fucked one. So I shall sound it over the roofs of the world, that which goes unspoken here, in this town, in the Orient's dark corner.)

Here. Here men have loved men. Sucked them fitfully and with grace. Made their love with them and fucked them at the hamam. Good fathers, good sons, good tutors: Turk, Armenian, Kurd. We accepted it and we didn't speak. We held our world of the hamam closely, tightly, a moving fist.

Now I coddle my cock and investigate masturbation and modern poetry. Can I masturbate and write at the same time? You will say I am an aberration. You will hate me. Give me your hatred. I'll hold it in my hand with this phallus. I can hold everything. It brings pleasure pain and gnarled sinew.

In the hamam, in the private rooms, we knew Sabit Bey's proclivity for the young boys and our teacher's love for an unveiled arse. Strong men became like their women in private. Men loved men. And for as long as the baths have existed men have performed their rituals. There is only one rule, and this is the rule I break.

As a boy I entered through the large wooden door with Hayrig. We entered passing Hamamji-Sinan and we entered the room of naked men. I shall never forget that first day at the baths, the day it was reserved for men. Did I know then? Did I begin then my battle against myself? Koharig pitted against my desire?

A room of odour and thick white air and a male secretion different from the women. Lounging languid men of all ages – the butcher, the doctor, my teacher,

158

the fixer, the coffee-server – together I saw them and there in the hamam they were different men, they were changed from the men I had known previously in the street and at school and in my home. They were men without women in private. They had removed their stiff coats and fezzes, their darned socks and thick woollen shirts; they had unwaxed their moustaches and fluffed their beards; they had braided their pubic hairs. They were naked men together in a room, with nothing but their forms to distinguish them: a pot-belly, a low-arse, short legs, rough feet. When the men removed their clothes they removed their families and their professions for the interlude. They left the central area and entered the private chambers and received massages; the very rich rubbed their legs against silk bath sheaths.

I dreamed of the girl Koharig. But that first day at the baths I fell in love with the form, with men free of their clothes and postures. Shall I pretend it never happened, as men here have always done?

Poem 2

My howls are no longer restrained, I'm the poet of this age – I'm the Armenian race rolled into a ball and stuffed into this attic hideaway, like an old blanket of snot.

Psalm 151

Praise the doo!
You deliver the weak
from their hoary pit.

But as for me, when I was sick
I wore a woman's dress,
I afflicted myself with books.

And they looked on in glee,
they gathered against me;
how long will You look on?

Give praise to your excrement,
maiden droppings –
they open wide their mouths to me.

Ala! Ala! they say,
we shall rescue you.
Praise the doo!

I have lost the ability to read. It's as if the words no longer make sense in my mind, no longer take me with them to the places that they travel. They're signs without meaning, black slashes and crosses and curled-up slants. I'm stuck here, in this lonely place, with these black marks. Is there any man lonelier than me, Sargis, writer of the Caca Poems? I've fast become the maudlin fellow I used to snicker at in school: Joseph the cross-eyed-boy who cried if you crossed your own eyes in front of him. Mary Mary! we used to tease him. Now I am Magdalene; my eyes are also red from crying.

I have given rein to passion and I have been estranged from the sovereignty of reason. Words fill my mind. I too am unrepentant.

Mama, I want to crawl into your arms again. Can you wrap them around me as you did when I was your youngest boy and you called me, Hokees! and you brushed my hair back from my forehead? You licked the snot from my nose. You picked the grime from my toenails. Now I eat mucus and toenail viands and I love it better than the viands you leave me: bulgur, apricot from the garden, cabbage and onion. Could you make me a snot stew? My fingers are in my arse and my nose and my mouth; for the first time I wish I were a woman so I could have one more orifice to plunder. I am an explorer in the new country of this body. Before perhaps I was taken with the idea of travelling abroad to Europe and to America, but now I know there is so much here: inside. I discover scents and dense pieces of myself. My fingers are restless. They dig in my arse, they cuddle my cock, they flick at my ears, they scratch my skull, they delve beneath my own toenails (do you see how I miss you, darling Mama?) and they always return to my nose, the centre of my being, and then to my mouth: I return everything to its source. I smell, then taste.

These corporal excursions free my mind. Small screams escape me, in air bubbles: You misled me to this, sons-of-whores, I burp. I could have spent my days in the garden screwing like a donkey. I could have turned my face to the sun for hours and hours every day; I could have looked directly into the sun's light, unafraid. I could have run down the hill as fast as possible to Mezre and Ambar Mahallesi Street. I could have stepped on a Turkish mullah's boot. I could have eaten gold.

You said, make plans. You said, here is History and handed me a leather-bound tome. You said, spreading your arms open and smiling with a sly grin: this is the way the world is. I never questioned the verb. I never peeked behind it.

Is shit.

Is my shit, my urine, my snot, my semen, spit, sweat, toenail grime, cream that collects in my foreskin, food between my teeth, oil on my hair, flakes of my skin, scabs from my arms, pus from the sores: I am.

Not you. Not you. Turkish Vali. Der Hyre. Professor. Policeman.

Professor Najarian, you saw the dark in your last tortured days, you showed me the horrible truth; you uncovered the lunatic place with your nakedness, its chaos and hate.

Only the viscera of the body comfort me. I pull my index finger from my nose; I suck on it. I have found good sustenance.

Mama came into the attic today and washed me as if I were a young boy.

Sargis, speak with your little-Mama. Hokees, my little-soul, you have said nothing in days.

She lifted my hands that cupped my sleeping cock and she raised my arms one at a time and wiped beneath them, deep into the hollow pits. She cleaned the sores on my forearms. She rubbed the wet cloth along my nape and along the curve of my back; her fingers fell into the hollows between my rib bones like a man soothing accordion keys. She smoothed my chest, my belly, the knobs of my knees, she drew the pearled cotton flannel down the length of my shin bones, into my toes and around my heels. She anointed me and I was not fit to be touched.

Mama then began to pick up the scattered bits of

food from the floor, the apricot pits, the ripped limp cabbage leaves half chewed. She sat on her knees, my mama, while I sat upon my stool staring up and out of the small blue window to the pretend world outside. I cradled my penis.

It's quiet these days, although no one ventures onto the streets much.

Mairig began to gather my scattered papers and books. She began to form two neat piles, one of books and one of my writing, and it was then that she noticed that many of the pages strewn about had been ripped from the books themselves.

My son, what have you done?

She looked very closely at me then and she began to weep. My stoic mama, who in the last few months, as so many have disappeared like so much boot-heel dust, has never shed the smallest tear in front of her youngest boy. She keened softly. She bent her head to the floor, she covered her eyes with her weary hands; she wore no rings of any kind. Everything is walking away from my mama.

I looked at her then, my dearest darkest mama, I pulled my gaze from the window, my hands from my limp genitals, and knowing how I still smelled, sensing suddenly my defiled scent, I opened my arms to the little bird in front of me: Mairig like a brown sparrow. Sensing my movement, Mama looked up and then she put her arms around my waist, she lay her head on my knees and the poor lady cried. We sat together for eternity: the Son and Mother. Our modern Pietà. I stroked Mama's hair from her head and I crooned to her.

I sang, It's time for bed, little bird. Go to sleep.

The world has become inverted and men are

women and the pious are heathen and evil is good and Jesus comforts the Mother of God. This is the world they lied about. What lies behind Is.

Tonight I am quiet inside. The roil does not take me up. Perhaps I could read but I don't choose to. I sit on my stool and I listen to the sounds of noise. There is no such thing as silence. When I am quiet it is the humming which fills me. It is as if all of the world's cacophonous jumble were coming from my inner ears. There is no noise outside of me: I am making the world. It is in my head. Sargis, Son of God. Mother of God. God.

I will never die. That is perhaps the most frightening of all.

The dark shines in the lightness, and lightness did not overcome it.

This is the final inversion.

I believe it is not within the Armenian consciousness to consider annihilation because, despite everything, all the long years of the cruel Turkish yoke, we have always survived. And what you cannot imagine you cannot fathom. And so, and thus, we are, after all, their easy slaughter; their quiet and unassuming and mostly docile slaughterhouse. We are their mewing lambs. Is that so?

What is this world for the human animal except a vast array of reasons?

There are birds but they are not the sound or the symbol. BIRDS. These are our ideas and our ideas are beautiful and filled with shitty mucus. They divide and unite and maim the unhardened heart.

And so, and so we die all the deaths on the earth, the deaths of all the ages. We die every single one of them. And we still would like to know, we ask ourselves and each other, why? And to what purpose? These thoughts fill our heads and make the world. These thoughts have no effect on the birds.

(And what is reason? And what is love? And what is life?)

Here I am still. Waiting. Counting. I'm immune to Mama even. She brings me food, she pleads. Two days ago, she tried to feed me using force. But I do not need food now, viands, nouriture, dinner, breakfast, supper, snack. I live from my words. I say, Urge and urge and urge, and I am replete.

Mama tried to stuff a sarma into my mouth as I crouched on my stool. As I stared up and out through my window, she thought I wouldn't notice the stuffed grape leaves she placed between my lips, past the portal of my teeth. I bit down hard on her fingers and she screamed when I would not release them.

Sargis! Sargis!

And I bit down harder until the knuckle in her index finger popped and cracked and burst forth in my mouth. I did not want her blood either. I released her.

Amot kezi. Amot. Shame on you.

My mama ran from the attic.

That was two days ago. Now when she brings me the food I do not touch, she leaves it by the hatch door. I can see a rodent in Mama's eyes now – it crouches around her pupils and it watches me. If I reach out my arm, it scurries away.

Mama has left me.

The flies have returned in droves. They fill up the attic. They abound. They rest in the sores on my arm.

Their translucent wings and black bodies have almost shut out the light in this room. They buzz and flit and stop to preen themselves. They set up appointments and have their backs washed. They are multiplying at an incredible rate. They eat my dinner, my breakfast and supper in a moment's time. They want more and more. I've stopped counting the fly eggs.

They want *me*.

Allofme.

And who am I, Sargis, writer of the Caca Poems, to say them nay?

Flesh of my flesh and blood of my blood, will you remember *me*? When this man, this Sargis, has become meat. Viands, nouriture, dinner, breakfast, supper, snack.

Hhuhhah.

Un Bon Gendarme

If he were asked he would not respond in this manner. Fear is a liquid burn. It has no beginning. In the stomach, behind the stomach and along the back and front of the spine up through the neck and into the ears. It spreads and reaches out further than that. It's not surprising. It never begins.

It will spread out and fill the body completely, up to the flats of palms and napes and arsehole, it forgets what it is. From this forgetting comes action. Actions large and heinous. These are the vile actions, the things that men do that make stories. Or uncensored epics. These are the stories that men never tell. The actions dissipate this filling-up so that he craves it, to be in action. He slices a man's ear off and for a moment he can hear above the din. A man's head is removed, the testicles are stretched and burned and *it* diffuses like light will on winter afternoons through a lattice window. When he's finished it returns and fills him up again. A hungry man devouring his share of meat. The fear fills him up like a liquid kiss – inner ears, behind the stomach, the spine. He has no idea that he is filled just as the body does not recognize the weight of its own blood. So complete he forgets. And in forgetting he is all powerful. He is not courageous. It is unnecessary – what could frighten him?

His ears are gorged so that he cannot speak clearly. He is the killer so that he can be the recorder and use language effectively. They call his names. They say, Please, effendi, Dear God, Please God effendi, Master, Master, Master. He can make men speak. His actions make men.

And what are men in any case? Shelves for storing food? Skin for holding an idea or two, a trade perhaps, a hoe? For curiosity sometimes he hacks with a particular order in mind. For each word they utter he takes a piece. The dogs cry: Dear God, Sir, Please Have Pity For Me, Son of God, Please, and it is (he breathes easily now, he is illuminated) eye nose hand foot ear ear leg arm foot leg arm heart in a pile. A man made into a pile. He looks at the mound he has created from a man and the rush comes and fills him again; kisses him like a woman. These embraces, his desire for the next man and the next. This one simply and cleanly: a bayonet slipping in. This man he pretends not to notice living among the dead heaps. He needs him to sneak back to town (he knows he will find him later); he needs him to tell the story. If the story is untold there is less pleasure, infamy.

Go little man, little Armenian boy. I'll get you. I know you.

He did not apprentice for this profession. As a child he planned to follow in his father's footsteps and work in his family's shop; they are a family of Turkish knife-makers. Sometimes he assisted his father and uncles and if he nicked a blade his father beat him on the face until he bled. His father taught him how to love the colour of blood. Slicing his fingers was an occasion of interest, how much blood could he issue? He'd stand and measure. He did not train to be a killer, but rather a craftsman in his father's shop. A maker. But does a man plan his destiny? He was the boy to try everything. He fell from trees and stone walls. He broke bones and cracked his head open. He fucked the sheep and goat and neighbourhood dogs. He collected his semen in small glasses. His father beat him with a natural rhythm for all of these misadventures. He craved his father's hands on his body.

He did not apprentice for this profession. He was raised in the poor village; he did not own shoes until the corpses yielded a thousand pairs. He carried a sickle and sowed eight varieties of wheat. His mother gave him bread and onions for his lunch and his father fought in the Balkan War; he patted his son's head before departing and reminded him of God's will. He was a sower. A boy with no shoes and onion sandwiches on warm afternoons. He fell from trees and stone walls. He broke bones and cracked his head open. He fucked the sheep and goat and neighbourhood dogs. He deposited his semen on the banks of the tributaries. At sixteen he married a girl with no name; he licked her adolescent breasts. He craved his father's hands on his body.

He was not apprenticed for this profession. He is the neighbour of twenty years. His sons and your child shot marbles together in the front and back alleyways; they climbed the trees in the garden and slapped each other's backs. He gave you the choice tobacco and you gave him choereg from your wife's kitchen. He said, My friend you are the gracious host. He was Effendi

Bey and his father before him was Effendi Bey. A man with leather shoes and the juiciest lamb kebab, he admired your beautiful knotted rugs. He came to your house for tea in the afternoon, he drank the tea and told a funny joke about the butcher. He fell from trees and stone walls. He broke bones and cracked his head open. He fucked the whores and he visited the hamam boys. He told funny jokes about the butcher and the winemaker and then he slapped your back. He said, My friend I will tell you a funny joke. He married the most beautiful girl with fair eyes and later he married again. He craved his father's hands on his body.

If he were asked he would respond in this manner: There was no beginning to my father's hands. He would not say, The body is heavy with contained blood. I can feel the liquid inside of me. He would say, I see things in the corner of my eye. A rodent, a hand, people coming behind shadows. Everything is a shadow if you look straight on.

As to Where are the Bootmakers and the Town of Kharphert

They set up a small bootmaker's stall at the edge of the commercial district and fabricated red, yellow, blue, violet and black half-boots, whose tips were pointed like a scythe. Within weeks everyone in the town purchased their boots at the modest and out-of-the-way stall. The lines stretched out for blocks. The other bootmakers went out of business.

Not long thereafter, the bootmakers set up a store in the bazaar and business increased exponentially as people began to buy shoes for the deceased as well as the living.

A red pair for my great-great-grandfather, effendi.

Yellow for my great-great-great-first cousin, once removed.

Black for my baby, sir.

Everyone in town swore that the quality and workmanship of the boots were unprecedented. Heretofore unknown in these parts. Never had the town seen or smelled such supple leather or fine craftsmanship, such vibrant colours.

There has never existed a more perfect pointed tip.

We could walk to heaven in this pair.

Perhaps a league or two further than that.

Eventually, the bootmakers bought out the west section of the bazaar (the shawlmakers did not even grumble at their ousting). The townspeople were on their sixth generation of antecedents by then.

Not long thereafter, the townspeople began purchasing boots for their descendants.

Two blues for my great-great-great-great-grandchildren and one yellow for their auntie.

I must have a black for my cousin's cousin's cousin's cousin's uncle's child.

People began to sell their personal belongings in order to increase their buying power. Ibrahim Agha was reputed to own three hundred pair, and counting. He was named Mayor of the town.

The bootmakers obliged the townspeople by accepting items in trade for their boots once the currency had been depleted. Hand-knitted shawls (17 per shoe), copper trays (15 per sole), bath sandals (in good condition – 10 pair per shoe; used and chipped unacceptable), clay urns (20 per heel), embroidered silk pillows (6 per pointy-tip), multicoloured blankets (50 per pair), and kerosene lamps (6 plus a tin of gas for a choice of boot colour) became exchangeable items.

Signs detailing the exchange values were posted throughout the south and east ends of the bazaar which became the bootmakers' waiting room and reservations area.

Not long after, the bootmakers agreed to accept gold

ornaments, family books, scraps of poetry, hoes, oxen, sheep, young daughters, chimneys, brick walls, tonnirs and land titles in trade. They expanded into the north section of the marketplace.

Ibrahim Agha lost his position as mayor when Joseph Agha traded his seventh daughter in for yellows, bringing his total count to 863 pairs and one shoe (violet). Joseph Agha's first declaration as mayor was: Long live the bootmakers!

His second item of business was a demand for more varied methods of payment.

Why not boy children also? he enquired. Wives? Laying hens?

Finally, (to the *Yeahs!* and *it's-about-times* of the crowd) preserves, sacks of chickpeas, bulgur, millet, local red wines, loaves of bread, stuffed cabbage, lamb kebabs, hunks of cheese, hens and boys under the age of nine were also accepted as payment. Combinations of items and what they could buy became increasingly complicated, and so Joseph Agha appointed Ibrahim Agha (up to 773 pairs and one blue and one black) Vice-Mayor of Calculations and Determinations and Worth as Pertaining to Foodstuffs and Material Stuff.

The town was torn down to make room for the expanding marketplace and to make overdue payments.

I'm concerned that red is becoming too popular these days, effendi. Perhaps a discount for the violet in the next few days? One oxen and one child, three sacks of grain and a case of wine as a small incentive to bring the numbers back to par?

Good idea Vice-Mayor of CDWPFMS. Excellent. Have I told you that I put in an order of blacks for my youngest son's niece five generations removed?

Later in the year, at the request of the voting popu-

173

lace, a new edict was issued (once the bootmakers had agreed on the content) concerning methods of payment.

As of today, 5 July, blumpty, blumpty, plucked out nails (in their entirety please, no slivers or scraps), pulled-out hairs (bulbous roots also intact please, this is a business), hands, fingers (allowable but of lesser value), feet (toes ineligible), fully intact soles, noses, breasts, testicles (with penis, an added pair), secondary internal organs (minus the spleen which can be given no exchange value), eyeballs (intact with blue given a slightly higher value) and all water sources will be accepted as official currency. Currency rates will change daily dependent on availability and circulation. Look for the signs in the Currency at a Glance in the north wing of the marketplace.

Soon red, yellow, violet, blue and black half-boots spilled over into the countryside. Surrounding villages heard about the boots and proceeded to the town and purchased in a frenzy. Before long, the entire region was bootfilled. The reds, yellows, violets, blues and blacks glistened in the sunlight. It was the most beatific summer in recorded history. The still-footed walked around saying, Beatific, isn't it?

The word *beatific* rose to the heavens until God himself, momentarily distracted from his game of chess, looked down on to the shining plains. He admired the rows and rows of red, yellow, violet, blue and black half-boots and he wriggled his unshod toes.

Gabriel, buy me a few pairs. Yellow, I should think.

When the townspeople's methods of payment began to dry up, the bootmakers looked up from their sewing and dyeing.

This always happens.

I agree.

A few weeks later they moved their business to an abandoned cookie factory in Munich and began refurbishing. They took in an ambitious street artist who quickly rose to the position of General Manager.

And three apples fell from heaven, one for the storyteller, one for the listener, and one for the eavesdropper.

11 February 1915

ക്ക്ക്ക്

We use language and words and books to try to ease closer to God. But we constantly move beyond reach and controlling. We strive and we heave the bracketed words together, aching to get in between their spaces, the hollows between letters and characters and sentence breaks and God and his children and the white white clouds leaning on a grey sky like a man against a limestone building. We are the women knitters. We weave and tear and knot hope for a moment's lexicon to reach towards the Holy. To make some thing lasting. So that you may touch it.

And we are always destined to fail. Miserable. This nation.

I will miss my children's brown and darkest blue eyes. My girls in a circle of three. My Karnik, the lion-hearted boy I sent abroad. He sits at his desk on the foreign shores of America and he reads the books in many languages. The boy I feared to keep here. The Western scholar.

Here I will miss the slanted tip of the thrush's wing. The college in winter, my students bundled against the cold and burying their fingers in the verses of Varudjian. The laboratory and the glorious 'X-ray' photograph of my wife's chest *cavity. And strangely, strangely I will miss the smell of the burned ash from behind the hamam. It reminds me of our halcyon days.*

I Am Nothing but a Girl

I am nothing but a girl from Erzincan. I no longer have
a body or swath of blue cotton for my hair. I am a girl
who walked with her mother out of her home, routed
from the hearth by a boy in a tattered uniform and
steel bayonet. Move quickly, infidel, the boy yelled,
and Mama and I began our journey. We walked to
the high walls, near the missionaries' homes. I carried
a knapsack and inside it dried chickpeas, wheat, apricots and flatbread. While we waited, the foreigners
approached us and offered words of grace for our journey. The one-legged cripple grasped the pious man by
his sleeve. Do not think that God has forsaken His
people, the foreigner whispered to him.

I spit invisible hate at the wind. I am nothing but a
girl. She spits hate. She doesn't wait for Christ. God
did not whisper in her heart. He did not say: I am here
to save you.

Shall I tell you about my mama? She's an old lady;
I am the last girl in a family of seven. My brothers

are taken. My sisters departed with their husbands' families. I pulled Mama along for days. Come on, Mama, I said, one more step, Mama. Move, Mama. Please, Mama. Move move move. Get up gettup.

You already know this story, you know the place in the wilderness where my mama fell down. The caravan continued moving forward, the whips and clubs of our guards smacked the mules and our backs. Our neighbours turned their heads from us as they passed.

Kna, Mama said to me, go with the rest.

To stay behind without the caravan meant bald exposure to the Turk men who looked and waited for the girls.

Kna, go on with the rest.

I sat down next to Mama. We didn't touch. Mama repeated one word over and over again: kna, kna, kna. Mama was spitting. Mama could hardly breathe. Mama whispered, Please go, please go away. And you know, you know this story. I stood. I caught up with my neighbours and I could hardly breathe, and they didn't look at me and I couldn't see the road or breathe. There were miles of dust. It made us invisible.

Do you know this place?

For days, timeless – we stopped knowing days from other markers. Without the end or beginning of time, we walked. The high ladies of our town always prided themselves. Their sleek dress and hair. The afternoon customs of tea and gateaux. The yes you mays, and the no you may nots. The tssk and the amot for every transgression.

Here they walked naked, hair askew, in the soot world.

They became bitter and fought one another for a hidden pocketful of grapes.

They screamed at one another; their husbands and fathers and teenage sons abandoned and finished. They clutched their small children's hands out of habit and rage.

At night the guards went through our ranks, ranks of women and girls diminishing, and they made their choices. Each night they pulled girls out by the hair or twisted arm, or they nodded and the girl followed; or the girl refused and the bayonet was thrust swiftly in the belly or breast. At night there was no wind, only the slap voices of the men and girls. They were behind the rocks or in front of me; these girls did not cry and old ladies pulled their hair and beat themselves with bared hands.

You lose your body like this.

The man uses his body and his weapons to lose it from you. His fingers, his hand and fist, tree branches and blade, his colleagues' hands and club. The vile body.

There are thousands of details and seven-year-old sweet-smelling children. If there is clothing, is it removed or torn? Does the girl lie on stones? Does the man? Does he open her dress, or slice the breast off in a fit of fury and hurry up? She is already naked, she has no shoes and her feet are torn. Her hands have ripped. There is a moment when the voice is vain, it runs out or slips out with the knife blade. Please please please. The djinn run amok in the night. They scream like Armenian hags.

Bitch bitch bitches, does he yell out? Or is he a kinder soldier? His dutiful penis, he doesn't look at you. He too makes you lose the body. You *know* this story. Have you heard or measured it? Who spoke it? With shame, did that girl bend her head? Or that boy? There were boys also in the dust, on the stones.

This is not me. I am a girl from Erzincan. I no longer have a body or swath of blue cotton for my hair. I cannot quote verse, I have not been schooled. I try to say this thing. But it is forbidden already. I will tell you, I will tell you: I spit invisible hate at the wind. I am nothing but a girl. She spits hate. She doesn't wait for Christ. God never whispered in her heart. He never said: I am here to save you.

We looked on. We did not participate. Mama, I called out. She is still beside the tree whispering, kna, kna, kna. There were no trees where I left my mama. Mama, I called out.

I'm not certain. I live with a man and his wives in Mezre; I was taken from the cemetery by a man. I was loaded onto an ox cart, I saw the blue skies above and Mama touched my cheek. Perhaps he noticed my breath, he unloaded me from the cart and Mama's touch. I clean floors and scrub pots. Not my voice but my breath took my mama from me.

I'm not certain. They would call me by my nighest name. Sometimes in this house they will slap me for an answer. I scrub the floors and I card the wool; I weave a new kilim. Who suckles the pitiful beast? There is an infant boy, he cries during the night. I can hear him. Who suckles the quiet child?

I am nothing but a girl from Erzincan. I no longer have a body or swath of blue cotton for my hair. Do you know this place? It stinks. My heart also stinks, like a ruined house or an animal that has died of disease. Perhaps I'm not really a girl, I'm stone. I am a stone from Erzincan and I lie next to my mama beneath cypresses on the road to the Der-el-Zor. My mama and I, we do not touch. She is also stone. She does not tell me to go. She does not beg or barter. She whinnies like an animal. She laughs like a stone. Granite. Marble. Grey and white limestone. The best homes are always built of limestone. Petrified. I'm not certain. I think we have died.

Five Garden Words

Why is it we are unable to mark the moments, except in hindsight, of inauspicious endings? Can you remember the last time you carried your father's slippers to him? You didn't know it was the last time, how could it have been in your mind? And so you don't have the image of your father receiving the brown woollen slippers from your quiet hands. Your guilt composes a song; it pervades the pores of skin and dips into every cell of the body. It reverberates inside of you. You should have known when you took Baba his slippers for the last time. You should have kneeled and kissed his hand. You should have stopped and made an etching in your mind, not run to check on the simmering fava beans.

After May, I slept because I dreamed of him. Of his hands and the cruel simple knotted rope. Of how his hands tired at their awkward position and of how they longed for streams of blood. How the longing was not for an untying, but for an untrammelling: blood flowing through its colourless canals, uncaught like a small bright fish released back into the water.

If they were to untangle him, I think, as I rise from my bed, he would be able to swim. I dream of Baba tied to Amo Berj, and of Amo Berj tied to Amo Hratch; of Baba, who followed his brothers as they followed him, eternally now. Into the waters. In a school of three. In my broken dreams I imagine that they are together. These three men. Like fish released back into the sea. A fisherman's unexpected kindness to the suffocating quarries. I imagine their uncaught blood flowing through colourless veins. Like wine into water.

Anaguil, bring me another.

Hagop sits in the garden smoking a cigarette. He raises his empty glass and waves it back and forth several times.

Iyo, Baba.

Anaguil stands up from where she is kneeling in the vegetable plot. As she approaches her father she notices his right hand moving slowly and constantly, tugging bead after bead along the chain of beads. An unstilled hand on black and white inlay. Worrying beads. The left hand holds the half-burned cigarette and the small glass.

This war will be temporary.

He doesn't look at his daughter; he inhales the black tobacco cigarette deeply. He has never spoken to her of things political prior to this moment in the garden. She nods and gently takes the glass from his yellow fingertips. She believes her baba when he makes that statement. The words comfort her as she walks through the garden, beneath the fig tree and its wide green leaves into the house.

Anaguil finds the bottle of raku in the cabinet and

184

fills her father's glass. She misses the days of school and the walking to the building everyday where she studied. She misses the gossiping with her friends, Rachel and Haigan; her father when he tells a funny story. Today she has come into the garden and begun to tear at the soil after the many months in the concealed house with the curtains tightly closed and the only music the step-stepping of the neighbour men on the rooftops as they made their way to the late-night gatherings.

The sun is shining and the snow has eased from the ground. This March is not as cold as some she can remember.

He lied. Her father of the thirty-six years lied like it was an after-dinner sweet, a small thing to appease the tongue. But even so, she persevered believing in his five garden words: This war will be temporary. She believed in temporary. In deciduous time, like the wings of a honeybee. But time lengthened. Moments replicated years and weeks became markers of for ever.

After Mama died in her sleep – it was a Wednesday, 23 June – Anaguil stopped sleeping past midnight and one and two o'clock in the morning. She awakened and she awakened again, so that the awakening seemed more like the sleeping. She remained with her eyes closed. Awake. At first she hoped that if her eyes were still then time would have the opportunity also to be still. Then Mama and Baba would be resting behind the bedroom walls, breathing. Then the step-stepping of the men would be the rain in the spring hitting the clay tile roofs and the heavy ground.

When Mama died she stopped thinking about

Baba's hands, Baba's fingers and hairy knuckles, his slim wrists. His swimming in the blue waters of Lake Goeljuk with his brothers.

When Mama died the world lost its breath.

Saturday News

Anaguil yegu, yegu from the garden.

Eh, Mama, Baba said to finish weeding the vegetable plots today.

Iyo. But come. Come quickly.

Anaguil gets up from her kneeling position on the dirt and walks into the house. Her mother has called to her from the second-storey window and so she climbs up the stairs to find her. In the bedroom, Yughaper is holding the family photograph taken that year by Armen. The boys and Baba are wearing their suits and she and Mama have their Sunday dresses on. They all stand around their seated Baba and they do not smile. They stare into the camera lens.

There will be one more soon. A girl. I'm sure of it. Yughaper taps her stomach. Anaguil looks from the photograph to her mother's hand resting on her belly.

You'll be happy with a sister, no? Another girl in this family is what's needed. She'll be nevart for the garden. A rose in winter.

Iyo, Mama.

187

Only Listen, Only Obey

❧❧❧

I did not leave Mustafa's home because I was weary. Or hungry, and could not bear another day of my mother-in-law, my sisters-in-law, or another day of seeing my children's thin-bone hands. Bread, Mama! Breadmama! they cried. They ceased their cries and moved listlessly or they did not get up.

We dreamed of loaves.

We hunted for it.

My mother-in-law said it was evil for us to walk in the streets unattended and while we foraged for food in the back alleyways of the marketplace, I wondered about the laws that kept us behind the kafe; later we burned the kafe to keep warm. We burned the windowsills and the inside door. We built fires with the dung we collected during the winter of 1914 when Mustafa and his brothers were fighting in the Russian mountains. I left in the early spring, after two of my girls died of the typhus disease, not to save the other girl or Timur, but to save *me*, Maritsa. I dreamed one night that my teeth had fallen out, my once-beautiful white teeth, and I have always wanted to live. The girl who wouldn't let the other children stand in front of the kafe. The girl who spent an entire day with her twin: Mohammed, Joshkun, Turgut. I was the best boy in class. I memorized each chapter twice over. I was the most devout. I was Yasar on my way to school, memorizing verses of the Qur'ān on my morning walk.

Selfish girl, they had once called me. Careless and idle; you look like a whore. I made myself into a man, I walked out of our home into the cold daylight. I walked on our street, alone, like a man. From habit, I suppose, my eyes followed the tips of my worn sandals.

Or is it fabrication, a girl's lie, this *me*? She left because she could not bear to witness another child's death: Güneli, Meltem, Nahit, Ratibe in a few months' time. The mother-in-law wanted them to stay inside and wait for the men to return, or for the Government to assist. And she refused to wait any longer. She dressed in her street clothes, she donned the veil and the mother-in-law began screaming, her cheeks puffing up and her bones clanking: What are you doing? Where are you going? Bitch. Ungrateful. She left before she called her whore. She kissed Timur; he lay unmoving on his blankets with his eyes closed, he hadn't risen in days, and the babygirl – the typhus disease was doing its work on their soft bodies also.

Later, when the mother-in-law began accepting Maritsa's money she knew she had won their silent battle of sent money and refusal. By late May, the mother-in-law no longer refused. Maritsa saw her at the hamam that summer. They didn't speak, but the old lady's cheeks were fuller, her bones not pushing the skin at hard angles. Maritsa knew her babygirl would suffer at the old lady's hands, but she turned her head and the hamamjee rubbed her calves.

I always wished to have been born a man. To slap the women. To beat them. I also would shove a bottle between their legs, or my fist, or my wooden club. To watch them wash my legs and prepare my meal, carry the heavy jugs of water on their thin necks and rise before dawn to light the fire and then fuck them. And yet, every man I have known has left me with only one desire: to lift my hand and bring it swiftly down on his face. I want to smash the faces of all the men I have known, beginning with my father, who sold me like a mule to Mustafa, who beat me with the same confidence. I have lifted my hand to caress or massage or carry a jug of water or serve the coffee. The men of Kharphert love Maritsa – her skin and smooth hands, her honey voice and square teeth. She's a beautiful girl. No one could have guessed that I'd become beautiful. Spotted mongrel. Bow-legged bird, my an-ne used to call me. The captain calls me a songbird. I sing to him; I make him sing.

I dislike the men for their stupidity, their wars of pride and bloodletting, their selfish and hitting temper. But as for the women, it is for their meanness, their pincing deathly meanness: they would beat the little bits of life from me. I left them, all of those women. From an-ne's house to Mustafa's – I never once had a moment to sit and to think, or to read a book. I envied the boys who schooled and who walked in the streets with a book in their hand, as if it were a view of the world, a new world: secret. I knew it was a foreign place, I could hear them speak from it: a foreign place in that thing which I looked at and it was nothing, dead for me. Why and how so alive for them? Only boys could read. I have been told that the Christians educated their girls, and only for this did I envy the gâvur. But they are so pitiable now, homeless and dying and hiding: I can smell their fear. I recognize it as I recognize my own.

She lives in a house with a few other women only a short walk from the hamam. The hamamji rubs clay on her back and removes the old skin with a loofah. The hamamji cleans her toenails and massages her back. Maritsa the whore gets a massage once a week at the bathhouse. She sees her mother-in-law and the two sisters-in-law at the hot water sink. They are fuller, they have recovered their strength enough to complain and criticize the smaller girls, the skin-and-bone girls. They are looking for a new wife for Mustafa. They search in front of her. Maritsa is dead for them. They speak of the first wife as if she were buried in the ground. But they don't speak of her at all. The first wife who buys their entrance to the hamam and the tourshi that they suck on. The first wife ignores them, of course, but for one word of Timur or the babygirl she would bend low. They know this. They keep their lips tightly sealed on the matter, the mother-in-law's special torture. The old lady takes the whore's money; she demands her payment.

When the war ends you won't hear about this girl Maritsa. If the men live they will come to find her: Mustafa or his brothers, or perhaps her own son if he has regained his strength. At night they will come, when she sleeps or works late. They will cradle her body, tilt her head back as one does with the sacrificial beast, the skin taut, and they will slice, swiftly, merci-fully. She is not afraid. She is not angered. As a man, she would do the same. This mark of shame cannot be tolerated. It is fact: she waits for this day with long-ing. As the military men pass through her room. *I am their meat already*. They lie on her, they lift her, turn her, stuff her: why was it not possible? She could have believed that the All Powerful made the smallest mis-take at her birth. She was the boy. She was Yasar on his way to school. An-ne said women were meant to suffer because Eve herself was weak. Eve, she said, was close to Satan.

Only listen. Only obey.

She did not obey skin and body. She imagined a rib that was not crooked when they spoke. She imagined it didn't need to be beaten straight. They will no longer beat Maritsa. They will tilt her head back until the skin is pulled taut, fair skin. Beautiful girl, beautiful mouth, she has unbroken teeth. Her an-ne didn't know she'd become lovely. A beautiful girl from a bow-legged.

This is what frightens her the most: Mustafa and his brothers may never return. They hear the rumours about the cold snowy mountains of Russia. They hear that the men have no food or clothing. They hear that the men die of the typhus disease more than the soldier's wound. She sees the soldiers in Kharphert and she despairs. Shoeless and clanky-boned they walk; the blood collects behind them like puddles after a rain. The hospital is filled, the hordes of tattered men linger in the doorway. Each one longing for bread.

She is begging you, she is praying to the All Power-ful: Come home, Mustafa. Come and slit your first wife's throat.

A Very Sad Ending

There was a town built on the top of a hill. There was not a town built on the top of a hill. There was another town located at the base of the rise. The twin towns, Kharphert and Mezre, were brothers, two suckling wolves; they had come from the same womb and drunk their milk side by side.

There was a terrible story about these brothers. A very sad ending. It was the sad ending that made the people in the towns the saddest people in the vilayet. From birth until death, down through the generations of townspeople, sadness was worn like a dull fez, or an old shawl in Kharphert and Mezre. People cooked their chickpeas in the saddest copper pots.

We will have an inconsolable ending, brother.

Ignominious.

Yes. Why fight it?

A man cannot fight his fate or his God.

The sadness intensified until a Wednesday towards the beginning of the century, or perhaps one day later than that, when it dropped its heavy load in the towns. In the form of an edict. In the shape of a decree. It

193

was a man's idea. Perhaps the man had been eating the last of his breakfast. Or perhaps he'd been wiping himself in a Constantinople washroom and his finger slipped through the ring of his arsehole. Or perhaps he'd been dreaming about an evening with his whore, Mayra, and the way she rouged her nipples. They are a problem. The Balkans were a problem, and see what happened there? Within a few years we lost everything. But this is no Europe, and not to mention that they're awfully close-close to those Russian Kazaks on the eastern border who wait for any excuse to take what is ours.

It had not become an idea until the man in Constantinople, a young man, slipped his finger (by accident he swore to himself) into that verboten dark aperture. Later that day in bed with his favourite whore, Mayra (her face buried in his posterior parts), he wondered out loud: Why, why, why not? Soon afterwards his colleagues confirmed: It's a solution of the first order, we suggested it last week. Mayra lifted her head from the crack of his arse and smiled, My darling, you'll be famous! Whereupon he pushed her head down again swiftly so that she could resume her duties.

A *why not* then determined the ending of the two brothers, the two suckling wolves. Of course others were affected, but this story is busy enough with one family. The man in Constantinople, a young man and yes, well, a military fellow, not too bright, but very bright-eyed, made plans. He liked to think of himself as a revolutionary and an intellectual (he repressed all of his memories of primary school and of the *professeurs* who made him wear donkey ears). He wore tailored Western suits and drank coffee in tiny hand-painted cups, he curled his moustache tightly on each end; he was convinced that the world would soon realize what a well-endowed and smart guy he was. Mayra, he called out, faster. I'm in a hurry to get back to the office.

With the idea (he opined it had not been inspired by the breached ring) came a few more ideas, some plans and even a department or two. Confidential memoranda were sent out statewide to all of the big head-honchos in the countryside. On occasion one of these head-honchos would ring up (if he could gain access to a telephone) and ask questions or perhaps even protest, ever so slightly. Sack 'em, the man in Constantinople, or his assistants or close colleagues would say. By then, there was a committee for the carrying out of the ideas that had been so nobly arrived at in the privy in Constantinople or in Mayra's special room.

Of course, it had been only one of many ideas that day:

Idea no. 1: Haemorrhoids are modern man's greatest travail; that puffy part itches.

Idea no. 2: Get rid of them.

Idea no. 3: The doctor's salve makes my arsehole itch *and* burn.

Idea no. 4: It's entirely true – my balls have switched sacks. Now the right one hangs lower than the left.

Idea no. 5: Mayra's thingy-down-there smells much better than my wife's – she probably uses special ointments or perfumes. Take a mental note: talk with wife *if possible*.

Idea no. 6: I've got it. Exactly: Get Rid of Them. Why why why not?

As fate would have it, the brothers in Anatolia had no idea what was transpiring in Constantinople. Or they simply couldn't believe it. Or they lay in the orchards sunning themselves and licking their pudenda. Or, it was an idea so strange and dark they confused it with one of the stories the old ladies whispered about on winter evenings.

The day came, however, when the ideas and the stories converged, the sad endings arrived for every last man, woman and child on a Thursday, Wednesday, or Friday towards the beginning of the century. One brother didn't have time to whisper to the other, I told you so. When all that remained of the towns were large white stones like prehistoric beasts and the brothers no longer figured into the local stories – they were lost or abandoned or burned, in short the two brothers who had once suckled the same milk never existed – then the sad ending was complete. But it was almost as if it weren't an ending at all, for how can you end a story which never is told?

Earlier, when the man in Constantinople heard the news, he looked up a bit surprised from his desk. Incredible, he giggled, what can a man think up next?

Silk

Anaguil walks along an unnamed alleyway clutching Ahmet's hand. She pulls him into a silent door and crouches down when she hears a muledriver behind her. The boy giggles and begins to suck on his fingers. Anaguil mumbles softly as she presses her back into the wooden boards of the closed shop. She is making lists of words and running through them again and again: *Harutiun's Bakery, confectioner, lavash, madzoon*. The wind picks up and muffles the clap of the mules' hoofs on the centuries-old packed earth. The muledriver turns onto a main street and the wind brushes Anaguil's skin. It seeps through the seams of the black çarsaf she is wearing, slips underneath the powder-blue headscarf and grazes her skull. It cools her, briefly. It raises myths. Ma-ma. Anaguil lifts her head, breathing deeply.

Anaguil pushes away from the boarded-up dry-goods shop and, pulling Ahmet alongside her, begins to walk again. Ahmet knows the routine and the favours he will win when they return home. He is quiet with his fingers in his mouth. She turns right down a small street. *Ma-ma*, she mouths.

In the distance, the cypresses sway and Anaguil can see their elongated green spears above the houses. She realizes then that the wind has beguiled her. It has used Yughaper's quotidian scarf to lift her mother up on a thin skein of the body's perfume. It is the blue heirloom that Anaguil has so carefully hidden from view beneath her full-length veil.

The trees and the air are still; the heat begins its work again.

Ahmet, one moment.

Anaguil bends to fasten her boot and she notices how the sweat drips from her elbows to her wrists and wets the cuffs of her dress and the çarsaf and her bootlaces; the hot sun makes her long for cool. For the now departed fraudulent wind. Anaguil lifts her head and looks ahead of her towards the well. She lists: *hot, sweat, river, sea.*

She panics. Today she cannot think of *silk*. Silky smooth and woven from the tiny bodies of white caterpillars for their own supple cocoons. Not such a long or complicated word. But common. Ordinary. She lists sheep's wool and linen and cotton and Kashmir. She can think of Kashmiri wool which she's neither felt nor seen, but only heard of. Her baba had admired it; he had lauded English Kashmiri coats: a European treasure, he'd said. But silk evades her. She knows *it*, but on her tongue there is only: *ipek*. No matter how she concentrates, it comes to her in that configuration only: ip-ek.

Auntie, I want two sweets this time. Do you hear?

Yes. Yes. Two. Haydi gidelim!

They recommence walking and Anaguil rapidly

198

makes more lists in her mind of other words, afraid they too will desert her. First textiles and then birds and then garden flowers and then simple household items: urn, bowl, cup, table, napkin, tablecloth, tray, platter, knife and spoon; and then types of trees. By the time they reach the edge of the quarter she is sure she will remember, it will sneak in quietly as long as she is not looking, like a mouse in the furthest corner of her eye. She will be saying: nightingale, eagle, sparrow, spotted dove, or: oak, cypress, evergreen, olive, willow, cherry-tree, and then it will come: silk. And she will make sure to memorize it. She will write it down when they return to Gülhan Hanim's house. In the largest letters. SILK in Mashtot's fifth-century letters. To make herself remember she swears not to use the word in Turkish. She will avoid it when speaking; she will talk around it. Perhaps that will leave the space in her mind's tongue for her Armenian word; for the girls in their rich embroidered shawls and smooth dresses and fancy bath sheaths; the women in her family as they once were dressed for mass on Sunday mornings at St Vartan's.

Auntie, one with sesame and one mulberry toffee.

Yes.

And next time we come to visit this ugly part of town, afterwards we will play marbles all afternoon.

Yes.

And I get tired when we walk too far. And I only want to go to the edge of the old quarter. Nothing there now.

Yes, yes, yes.

Anaguil tucks her head tightly, she clutches Ahmet's hand. They walk briskly toward the old Armenian quarter. They will only stand on its edge. She will only look briefly. The child is correct: there is nothing. And she has told Gülhan Hanim that they will be home before the afternoon meal.

Postscript Found

Hakan. This black place I'm in. This black place I'm in. I could have been your sweetheart girl.

There's no leaving, you understand. A living man cannot hide his body. This flesh confines me, a man made into a woman. The fucked-one, Hakan. Your summer tendril, cuneate leaves; poetry and the wide sky. Their passive witness is bitter.

We are together in a garden and you hold my hand and you lick my cheeks; my tears run down like Mary's. You slip my pants from me and I open my legs for pleasure. I would have been a woman for you if you had allowed me. I was a female man in your arms. I opened my legs for you and waited, a smile on my red lips. It is the most unreasonable thing. My love for you. My love for a Turkish boy whose hair flies into his eyes like a woollen cape. Where have you left your red fez, darling?

I am writing you this letter.

Dear Hakan, it begins

Or, Dearest Hakan

Or, My Sweet Hakan

Or, My Love for You
Or, Bastard
Cur
Evening Poet
Or, Soldier
Or, Effendi Bey, I kiss your boots, I clean your heels; I suck your fingertips and polish your rings. Where are you now?

Iyo: I miss you; long for you. A man-woman in an attic writing a letter to his lover who never was his lover. We stood there together at the edge of love – Turk and Armenian. For centuries. We stood by that terrible, black place.

Hakan, my dear, are you killing? Are you being killed? Do you eat sedge from the banks of the Bosphorus? I have been told that Constantinople is a beautiful city, the Armenian architects left their mark here and there. You can smell the sea air, the ruckus gulls lift onto warm currents; a stone wall divides this plot of land from that one over there.

These things in my head I give to you. These things in my head I unload before it is impossible, and they remain stagnant, sticky, buried in bodied cells and body meat, the flesh of this flesh. These are things we never spoke of. Perhaps I cannot recall everything. You with your mind's weight can close the windows. Eh, my friend?

Hakan, it begins, this is a very black place I'm in. I could have been your woman. Washed your feet and prayed for you five times a day. There were no limits to this Love. A Love without hope. A Love without Reason or History. Prohibited. The dangerous kind. The most terrible possibility among men, our Turkish, Kurdish and Armenian men. My greatest trans-

202

gression? Choosing you and longing to lick your back.

We will die in this war, Hakan. You and I. For me, an ignoble death. Beheaded. Sliced open. Deposited in an unmarked grave. Food for the roaming and picking dogs. My name and the clan, buried. Burned up. Ffft. Becoming transparent smoke.

For you? Sliced open, they slice your boots off of your feet. They are so swollen, there is no other remedy. They leave you on an alien road beneath the trees – this is the march to the Dardanelles; the men call out down the line of marchers that a sick man lies beneath the trees. The horse-drawn cart passes by you and abandons you there; the sergeant says, Make room for the living. An unmarked grave; Aziz Bey will never find you. Noble death. A martyr's death. A monthly pension will come, the ninety-nine kurus from the Government can buy your family six loaves of bread. I think your mother will spit on the coupon book.

I won't see you in your Heaven.

These words will keep all gates closed to Sargis.

The monks and teachers and pious will burn me. They will have me ultimately. My head on a stake. The beloved will be fucked, the greatest screw of all time: my head for them; a trophy they'll give to Mairig. Madame Terzian, they'll call out in the street, take this piece of your son home with you.

I'll stick my tongue out for eternity. And clean the black milk from my plate. Iyo.

I sign this letter fitfully in the darkness. Goodbye, darling. Ah, I'm a romantic sod. To God, then. But whose? Sorrowfully, with sorrow – these never did end epistolary communiqués. Inşallah.

Inside, 1917

Anaguil wakes up bleeding. And it is as if all of Kharphert flows from her in tiny and big clots and flows and viscous threads of blood and body blooded. She cries. She says, Mama, I am no stoic. And she wipes her index and middle fingers into her vagina and she lifts her fingers and she smells and then tastes. And although appalled, she loves her blood's taste, its brine lead in the mouth reminding her of knives. She loves the taste of body in her mouth.

She asks herself inside of her self, alone with her own flesh and her flesh bleeding for the first time in two years, a small question, a question she has heard in the past years more than once as doubts pile up like girls, their braids suspended into the depths of the well like reaching hands; she whispers in a corner of her thinking, softly, unobtrusive like the hanging corner spider, she does not move: Where is He? Jesus?

And she thinks, I am sixteen now: old enough to marry, to have children, to sew beautiful shawls and coverings, to make lavash and kifteh and cured sweet-meats. She sucks her fingers.

*   *   *

Don't be stupid, Haigan says.

But it's awful, this work. It makes my eyes water and my fingers ache, aching to run outside.

It's what every girl must do well. How else will you fill your hope chest? Who else will embroider the towels? Or create the lovely lace edges for the pillowcases, sheets and tablecloths?

Anaguil looks at her closely. Is this what we're good for, Haigan? This machination of hands like little water mills? These arch rosettes on white linen?

You want to be a good wife and mother, don't you?

Mr Davis Departs

❧

Mr Davis departs Mezre today. He is leaving with the
Mr Riggs, Mrs Atkinson, her three children, Miss
Campbell and three other American missionary ladies.
All of the Americans are leaving today with their possessions loaded onto their five covered wagons. They
are nervous and scared on account of their journey
overland. Eight trembling travellers load onto wagons;
the men will ride the provided mounts. Each one holds
his papers of citizenry tightly in his fist. They worry
that the papers will not provide adequate protection
in the wilderness. The police escorts are mildly amused
by the nervous manners of their entourage; to pass
the time they smoke cigarettes and make whispered
boasts about the unequalled sexual prowess of Turkish
bulls.

I did not see them leave. I have heard from others
about their journey out of town. Hundreds went to
usher them off and bid them goodbye. Hundreds but
not all. The trees in the Consulate orchard are no
longer crowded with exiles. We do not hide the men

and women from Mr Davis when he takes an afternoon stroll in the garden, the men and women that
were never on his rosters. During his time at the Consulate, Mr Davis kept a card index of our names locked
in his desk, our name and next to it our relation to
relatives in America: official document. Without it, we
could not remain behind the high stone walls. Officially.

These people, how ignorant they are, he once told
me. They have no clear notion as to their correct sur-
name. Any one person may have five names or more.
Some adapt the Christian name of their father and add
ian – father is Hovaness and they are Hovanessian.
Some of the village ladies add this *ian* to their husband's name; some people use their grandfather's
Christian name; some will give me their name translated into English. It's a bookkeeping nightmare, Lucy.
It makes it quite difficult to keep an orderly card index
under these circumstances.

The children are not learning their numbers or
English phrases on the third floor. I have heard
that the Kaimakam will make the Consulate his new
home.

Many people from the orchard and from the rosters
escaped to Russia with the help of the Dersim Kurds.
Some children are with the Germans in their orphanage and others are with Miss Petersen in the Danish
house. And this girl? This Lucine? Was she able to save
her brother and send him to America? The Amerigatsi
assured me: I will take the US nationals with me
when I depart. I will make every effort for you. I
love you, he whispered. The weeks passed and he
penned his reports furiously. When he began burning
papers, when he and Garabed burned all of the papers

in the Consulate, then she knew it was forsaken. Before he departed he gave Garabed some photos of the lake, a typewriter and an engraved writing utensil. Garabed whispered to me in the hallway, He is leaving us here.

Days arrive that would seem unarrivable.

Mr Davis did not sleep during the final days of his stay in Mezre. I waited for him, I was prepared for him even at the end. He did not come to me. The day he began burning his papers he told me: I have found you a house two blocks from here. Your brother will be safe with the Germans. He said, I will send for you, my dear.

When Consul Davis left Mezre on his horse I was washing the clothes, I was mending the hems, I pounded the chickpeas. I was still. My hands moving or my arms, and I was still. He gave me money from my father in America. My father who is not my father. My father who was my classmate's baba – she and I shared the same first name. She had a beautiful younger brother who climbed trees in their garden; her saint's day was mine also. My namesake, she used to say. My namesake, I'd reply smiling. God has a special plan for us.

Lucine departed on the road to Mesopotamia. Lucine made a path to Mezre. Mr Davis rubbed my arms and kissed my neck. Lucy, he said, I will always remember you.

In Mezre there is little bread to be found. From chickpeas I make biscuits. My brother stares at me through the windows of the German missionaries' orphanage. He cries for his mama. We do not know when this war will end, or what the end will bring us. There are things we do not tell anyone, there are children we cannot name.

I live two blocks from the American Consulate with four other ladies, ladies I used to work with in the kitchens. They despise me; they barely tolerate my presence. I look up and out through the window when I am sure he and his entourage have passed, I press my stomach: it is empty and filled. I think of their journey. They will leave Mezre and head towards Eregli where they will take the Railroad to the Capital (I have never seen this modern machine which travels on metal roads). They will go to Europe and then they will go to America. So easily their persons will travel with the papers that allow them to move away from Mezre. I try to make biscuits from dried chickpeas. My belly is empty and filled and we are hungry all the time now. The ladies I used to work with in the Consulate kitchens will not look at me. They don't speak my name, they speak about me as if I am not here.

That girl is a shame to our race.

Sodom and Gomorrah.

That girl will suffer the wrath of God.

Whore.

I am sick these days and my belly is filled when it is empty. I don't think my namesake would recognize me now, a thin-bone woman with a belly beginning to protrude. I wonder when this war will end and what the end will bring us. Mr Davis departs on 16 May 1917, a few months after his country entered the conflict. I hold my breath, I am still. I don't see him leave and he does not see what he leaves behind. I have money enough for two months, perhaps three if I am frugal. Bread is more expensive than silk these days.

Removed

꧁ ꧂

Ismet enters the front door bearing two wooden
trunks. Gülhan Hanim follows closely behind him saying, I'm looking for cloth, copper pots and woollen
rugs. Nishan looks silly, as do Stepan and Jirair, in my
old hemmed dresses. I thought we might walk
together from the house, but Ismet says no. He drags
the two trunks into the salon and opens them. Here,
he says, we will put the children here. I will walk out
from our home with my small bundle and some loaves
of bread, the children will travel inside the trunks.
Gülhan Hanim is pretending to be a buyer. We will
pile linen on top of the children. I was worried Nevart
would cry, but she is no longer crying. She knows.
She has learned.

Ismet loads our precious trunks onto the transport.
Other Turkish women and men load furniture onto
their wagons, or they carry their items on their backs.
The gendarmes appear and disappear. I am the last
person to leave the house. I wear the black çarsaf and
I shut the front door to our home. I lock it out of spite
and pride. The bedding is neatly put away inside the

cupboard. I scrubbed the floors the evening before, Nishan whispering mad at my back, Are you cleaning for those dogs? But they would not find us unclean or slovenly. I scrubbed the floors and I burned the last of Baba's papers – I'm not sure why, but it seemed better than leaving them for their perusal. There is a red bloom on the rosebush in the garden, a late and latent bloom.

I don't want to remove my hand from the door handle. Come, I say to my fingers, and they obey like good children. I can see myself standing in front of the door to our home, I think I shall always see myself there, my hand releasing – a Turkish girl in a full-length veil pulling her arm back from the door at the threshold of our home. Permanent as a photograph. My back to the wagon and Ismet and Gülhan and the two trunks of our silent and dark family. I see myself turning away, my back to our door, my feet moving me from the threshold and the lintel and the possibility of return. We shall never return, I'm sure of this thing. There are some actions which provide no return.

They wait for me, the boys and Nevart wait in the darkness of walnut. I perspire inside the black veil. I cannot breathe evenly. I take in large breaths of air. Beads of sweat run down my cheeks as if I am bleeding. Now, I say. Now I will die from this. I turn and walk to the wagon. Ismet helps me up and I sit next to him, Gülhan Hanim says to me in Turkish, We still need some kitchen utensils. We make a stop at one more house and Gülhan Hanim buys a copper pot from the wife of Setrak Ailanjian, the dentist. Madame Ailanjian does not recognize me in the black veil. I don't look at her but keep my gaze on the floorboard of the wagon. Gülhan Hanim does not haggle. We hurry after that. We drive to the other side of town. A mixed neighbourhood of Turks and Kurds and a few, bartering Armenian. Ismet carries the trunks inside. The boys jump out and ask for water. Nevart has fallen asleep, her lips pursed like a bow. She also is covered in perspiration.

I Was Mama's Rose

The cotton folds smell of her, the heavy sounds of a hundred feet marching like dumbeg music in the dark. Chhhht, Brother says to me. Mama, Mama, my reply. It is quiet and my sister tells me, or Mairig kisses my tongue quietly. I'll slap you. Later with the back of my hand, pull your tongue out.

They lift us high like topsy clowns. Chhhht Chhhht they say from inside my chest. Mama's gone and the cotton smells like Mama and the heavy sounds of marching are like drum beats.

Chhhht or the djinn will take you, the Devil, Turk.

Through walnut, the light slants their voices and a child inside a trunk: we're going to our new home, Anaguil says. You know how to hush now.

My brother plugs my mouth with his metal fingers. Chhhht Chhhht. Mama, my reply, sucking his digits like titty. Seeking milk to fill the hole in my chest.

They lift me from inside and place me on the floormat. I walk again, I see window light, cushions to sit upon. A little boy peers from behind his mother's legs. Your name? I say. He hides. Ahmet, my sister tells me. Ahmet is five years old.

What's my name?

Dilek, my sister says.

Dilek Dilek.

The Djinn of Ras-ul-Ain

My favourite dish was no dish at all, rose-petal preserves on fresh bread. Mama would make it in summer. I remember we'd eat jam, we'd see the groom's
family come with the hennanoum to paint the fingers
of the bride for the henna ceremony, we kissed our
father's hand, the Der Hyre's hand, our teachers' and
uncles'. Kiss-kiss.

I am always forgetting. I am disorganized and I have
little to say. I walk continuously; the walking makes
me forget. I am disorganized with my thoughts. I tap
people on the shoulder. I breathe in their ears. They
shiver and I am afraid. It's as if there are no days, no
form. I am disorganized. Aman! I say.

When we began to menstruate we used special rags.
Often my back and my kidneys ached until I cried
and Mama would come smiling, Preserves and bread,
hokees? I know we ate sweets on such days.

We went to school and we made the most beautiful
needlework. I embroidered a pillowslip with golden
birds and lilac for my hope chest. As a small child, I
wanted to become a doctor and my sister Haigan made

fun. Silly! she said. Girls cannot study medicine. When the hennanoum came to our house and painted my fingers I laughed even though I was afraid.

What did Artin say? Goodbye, dearest wife.

> No. His pants marked with urine, his eyes a hollow place. Serpouhy! he called out, as if my name could comfort him. I had the babe in my belly, the girl clung to my legs. Perhaps he said nothing.

At the moment of leaving, fear, not love, speaks loudest.

They ordered us to remove our garments. Our clothes were dirty and torn, mostly beyond repair. They tossed them into different piles: what could be salvaged, what was to be burned, a small mound of gold and jewellery, the last pieces that somehow had evaded their searches in the past months. I approached the soldier. A man from Diyarbakir or Mardin. They used their fingers to look for lira.

> They know all of our hiding places, the woman next to me warned: hair, the hidden hems, vagina. The safest place, she whispered, is the rectum.

They yanked the coins and rings from our bodies. They smelled their fingers and laughed.

> This man used his fingers, that one a knife or sabre.

When my first child was born, she was sickly. I feared she would die of disease. I kept watch over her. I fed her, touched her and I prayed. She improved with time and soon she could lift her head. I remember when she smiled at me for the first time, the happiest moment for a mother! I laughed with Artin at dinner. We were relieved. It's a good omen, he said. Already, he was planning for a son.

I fight against the forgetting, just as I used to fight against sleep. To be lost in the world of sleep without form or my body always terrified me. Forgetting is worse than losing the body.

We left Kharphert on 5 July with the rest of our quarter. We camped on the outskirts of town that first night. My daughter cried for her baba. I fed her some bulgur and dried apricots. Haigan said, Serpouhy, how is the babe? I touched my big belly.

Haigan was bent at the waist when the man on horseback flew by. He grabbed her plaits and dragged her with him. She screamed. What did she say? Serpouhy, don't let him take me! Serpouhy, what is happening to this world? Serpouhy, how can Turk and Armenian live together again? I can't say. I could never be sure what Haigan said, her destination. One moment she was leaning over, bent at the waist. Her back ached from carrying the bedding. How many weeks or months had it been? I can't say. First, she bent over, or perhaps she was standing tall, not ten feet from me. She was saying, Serpouhy, my arms ache and my feet have torn.

> The old lady sold her granddaughter for a pouch of millet.
>
> Mama, when I die, you eat my flesh. Do not share it with anyone.

The Christmas holidays with my relatives were my favourite time of year. We'd eat from afternoon till night: raisins, figs, apricots, rose-petal preserves on

Mama's kata, the most delicate baklava. Cookies of every variety: sesame, date, butter, poppy-seed. The boys in the quarter sang songs from the rooftops and dropped their wicker baskets by our front windows. We filled them with pastries, dried fruit, toffee. They sang louder and Father God was everywhere.

Aman, I say.

The body is nothing more than a question. Will you slice this breast? Will you take this hand? The body lies in wait, vulnerable, unrhetorical. Along the road to Ras-ul-Ain, as we neared, we saw piles of hands.

It is the children's voices I hear above the din. They call out for their parents, eternally. Ma-ma, they say. Ba-ba. Come for me.

Two of them grabbed my arms. One held his sabre high in the air. He had long eyelashes, a dimpled chin. He said, A gâvur's disgusting progeny. A man with long eyelashes and a dimpled chin who slices my belly open wide, like a mouth. He reaches inside with sabre and pulls the babe out, holds it high and laughs: a gâvur's disgusting progeny. The umbilical cord makes a popping sound like a cork being pulled from a bottle.

I am already forgetting. I am disorganized and I have little to say. I walk continuously, the walking makes me forget. I am disorganized with my thoughts. I tap people on the shoulder. I breathe in their ears. They shiver and I am afraid. It's as if there are no days, no form. I am disorganized. Aman! I say. They do not hear me. I wander in the desert toward Ras-ul-Ain. The Bedouin build fires around me, they pitch their tents, on special occasions they slaughter the lamb. I am always unable to reach Ras-ul-Ain. I am lost, I forget and I am disorganized. I am forever hungry. Ravenous. I wear a necklace of small and large hands.

The Commander Says I Am His Favourite

ೲೋೲ ೲೋ

I hold him in my arms and he begs me, Suck my titties.

Our Minister of War buried his face in my posterior and cried like a babe.

The man licking my back sent Mustafa to Russia; he sent all of the farmers to die. No wheat, no bread. There are no Turk men to seed the fields; the Armenians are gone with their awls and skill. Who will make our boots? Who will sow the wheat? The baker was killed, the furrier rests in the central square. The tailor, tilemaker and the carpenter will never return. Mustafa is not returning to Kharphert and who will kill me?

I have seen the women and men in town wearing new clothes. They cook in new pots, they sew with new needles and cloth. They lie on new cushion and rug. They burn the doors and windowsills of empty houses in winter. They say, Maritsa is the whore.

All of their things are still in this town. The bodies are departed. The spirits unanchored now. Their spoons dipping into the child's bow mouth. I wonder, will they all return to haunt us?

Who will be the culpable one?

The man licking my back, sucking these titties (there is no milk in this girl); the man who buried his face in my posterior and cried like a babe?

Who will sow the wheat field?

I don't let the servant boy buy the infidels' things. Why not? he asks. It's a good bargain. No and no and no. I know what strange spirits lurk inside metal and wood and cotton swaths. There are piles of clothes at the marketplace. My neighbour has a new mauve dress, it is tight at the bustline. Toes ache in the too-small boots. Someone is learning to play the 'ud, the boys throw the dice on the backgammon boards.

But who to sow the wheat field? And who to tan the hide? And who to fix the watches?

This town is the whore.

If God has no pity on them, why must you have pity?

They deserved their fate, they were all political agitators.

All gone, all dead.

There is no room in the Empire for Armenian and Turk. Either they had to go, or we.

Liberty and equality are not to be pursued by the infidels.

They can live in the desert, but nowhere else.

Unfaithful. Disloyal. Saboteur.

I go to the hamam and the hamamji wipes the clay from my back. The Commander says I am his favourite; he whispers to me in the night. You smell of lilacs, he says. Our Minister of War stayed in town for only a few days. He arrived in an automobile and people lined the streets to see the modern travelling machine. He was a not-too-tall man. A man of plans and ideas. He talked for hours and hours, formulating his plans, as if I weren't there. He spoke loudly throughout the night.

When I was a girl, my An-ne warned me how my thoughts could be the death and corruption of me. A woman should not think, she'd scold. Honour and obedience. Not think. Only listen.

All of my life I have had only one desire: to bring my hand down on their faces: the men and the women who have directed me. They directed every action, the smallest desire, since the day of my birth. And I have always been an indomitable girl – a girl with ideas.

Instead, I sing to them. I make them sing.

It's as if I am not here at all. This *me*.

My Final Report

I have been home for three months now. I am working on my final report to the Consular Service of the Department of State. I stay up late into the night writing. Catharine tells me I must sleep more. Your eyes are red all the time. They look horrid, she says. Horrid.

I have seen many hundred Armenian *émigrés* since my return to America. I make the rounds to different relief and community organizations in New York and Worcester, Boston and Providence, and they make inquiries regarding their relatives and friends. I have told them what I know and they thank me for my assistance on these matters. There is no current news from Harput and Mamouret-ul-Aziz and we all wait to discover the outcome.

A boy came to see me this morning. Somehow he ascertained the location of my private residence at Port Jefferson. Our houseboy led him to my office, a young man in his early twenties. He was dressed in a three-piece suit, he was clean but ragged in his features. Before I could shake his hand he began assaulting me

223

with questions. Your name, sir? I demanded. Karnik Najarian, he said. I am the son of a professor of philology from the Euphrates College at Harput. Until quite recently, I was a student at Cornell University. I must know, he said.

Sit down, I told him. I will ring for tea. Would you like tea or coffee perhaps?

What has happened to them? he continued, ignoring my hospitality. I have had no news. For almost two years I have been making inquiries at all of the agencies in Constantinople, Harput, Mezre, Tiflis, Aleppo, Ras-ul-Ain. I have heard nothing. I have abandoned my studies, I cannot think and I cannot study. What is the reason? My father, my mother, my three sisters.

Sit down, I told him again. Please have a seat. Let's have tea or coffee. I'll tell you what I know.

He stopped talking then and began shaking his head from side to side. More and more vehemently, as if demented, he swung his head back and forth. He lifted his hands in the air and his eyes to mine. They were dark Oriental eyes, frightening in their intensity.

I'm sorry, young man, I told him, and with my sorry he collapsed. Not physically – the boy remained standing. He dropped his arms. He was a handsome lad for one of his race. I saw his eyes collapse.

I'm sorry, young man.

He turned abruptly and walked from my office, no reasons but he had found his answer. I sat at my desk again and attempted to continue my final report. I can't get that boy out of my mind. I see his eyes, dark and unfathomable. Horrid. I ring for tea. I will have tea with a dollop of cream. I'm tired, Catharine tells me I must rest more. She tells me it is time to focus on our family and to think of children, the modernization of our home, an extended vacation this summer. These past years have been strenuous ones, there was never an opportunity to spend the hot summer months camping at Lake Goeljuk as my predecessors had been in the habit of doing. I was rarely away from the Consulate for more than a few hours at a time. I am terribly fatigued. They understand. At the Consular Service of the Department of State they understand that for three years I laboured tirelessly under trying circumstances to protect American interests abroad. I carried out my duties in accordance with the expectations and obligations of a man of my position. All this I do solemnly avow I did to the best of my abilities.

Upon filing this report, I shall take a few days away with my wife. We will travel a few hours north to visit some friends in the countryside. I am fatigued but sometimes late at night I find it is impossible to sleep. I am afraid to dream. It is my hope that in the next few months I will recuperate fully.

Inside, 1917

There are days I cannot speak. Each word is a weight, and there are pounds of flesh, the heft of diction. I say good morning and I am wearied. Good morning pulled from the body, from my mouth, like opaque stones. On these days I say little to Gülhan or Kara, I do my chores, I knit, we clean, perhaps I will stare out the window after the evening meal has been prepared. Gülhan leaves me to say little as I work; she does not press me for words, this woman who has become my auntie in the past one year and nine months, who has held my family in the cup of her hands. I give her our weekly payment, there are months of gold payments; I move but I cannot speak – in language the burden lies heaviest on the dark days.

My words might have been: When will I marry him? I love you from the lovesong. Your shoes, your coat, the dark-tipped eyes. Mama, is the bride the most favoured? Mama, does a girl ache? Can she speak?

In the time before, there also were days when words were heavy and pulled out from the body as if from stone. I was angry at my baba, the way he berated Mama; the constant streaming of chores; the be a goodgirl, don't fidget girl, clean your nails, plait your hair, do your stitches anew. But when those days were finished, speaking again was light: I didn't notice language as I didn't notice my own breath. A girl who marvelled and chatted with Rachel and Haigan in the afternoons, who sang with Mama in the garden.

I remember how Murat Agha used to come to our home for tea. He loved Mama's baklava and swore that no other Armenian woman could prepare it so well. He would come into the salon with Baba and I would serve them their tea, their baklava, and they would smoke and later drink raku. The room filled with their smoke and their talk of sales, purchases in the capital, how the Vali would drive all businessmen to ruin with his taxation.

Murat Agha was not as tall as Baba nor as fine; he had a long nose and he used to joke how he loved food like he loved commerce. His cheeks turned red in our home and his red fez lay by his side. I brought in more tea, more baklava, or cheese and olives, or meat pies. They lay on the cushions and they smoked and the last time he came to our home, they both held their worrying beads in their hands. I did not see his red fez at the crook of his elbow.

Murat Agha and Baba were partners for fifteen years. Baba stood up at his wedding and Murat Agha came to my christening at St Vartan's. They took tea together, they drank raku. They travelled once a year to buy goods for the shop. For fifteen years Baba went to the store each morning. He rode atop the mule or he walked the short distance to the bazaar. He wore his black suit jacket and his polished boots. His moustache curled on each end. He opened the shop with Murat Agha in the early morning and they drank coffee and they sat on small stools and they kept their inventory in check: handmade rugs from Bozmashen, copper trays, pots; silver pitchers, and silk shawls from Sivas. They spoke Turkish and when Murat Agha would hear us speaking in Armenian he would say, Eench-spesez, Anaguil? the words we children had taught him as an amusement. Mama spoke Turkish poorly; she had never been schooled and at home and in the quarter it was only Armenian. We children translated for her when the town crier passed by our corner: War, Mama, there is war on the waters.

After Baba was taken, Murat Agha kept the shop open. He sat on his stool by himself, he drank the coffee from the coffee-boy, he wore his red fez and he chatted with the knifemakers. The shop remained open throughout May and part of June of 1915, the last year of the last life we had together. The goods were never confiscated by the Government; they remained in Murat Agha's possession: the silk shawls, the copper trays, the silver pitchers. Sometimes I think about our property: if you pour honey from Madame Ailanjian's silver urn will it turn you bitter? If you admire Madame Minassian's silk rug will it make you grave? I gave Mama's silver tea service to the tile-maker. Her great uncle had given it to her on the day of her marriage. When the tilemaker takes tea does he think of the Armenian girl who shoved the silver service into his hands? She wouldn't sell it to the Kai-makam's wife; she saw the Kaimakam's wife heading her way with a buying gleam in her eye.

Murat Agha sends letters when he can. He says he

will be home soon. I read these letters to Gülhan as we sit around the tonnir or in the garden and she darns Ahmet's trousers. Like Mama, Gülhan has never been schooled; I read her his letters five and ten times. Read to me again, Fatma, tell me when he returns.

It has been more than one year and nine months since Murat Agha went off to war. He writes that war will be the end of the Ottoman Empire as we have known it. I peer into the looking-glass and I see a girl of sixteen who cannot speak today. She opens her mouth like a bird and she remembers Hanik. She wishes she could sing, the words to a lovesong go round and round in her head. She would step outside of herself, open her mouth, flatten her throat and warble: Mama, why did the world lose its breath?

When Murat Agha returns to Kharphert he will find us in his home, the two Armenian girls he has adopted. Fatma and Dilek. A girl with a too-thick nose and a blue-eyed darling. Gülhan doesn't speak to me of marriage; she doesn't speak to me of changing our faith as we changed our names; she knows I can't bear it. She speaks to me instead of stitches, special embroidery patterns, how to make the best kifteh in tomato broth; the ailing soldiers in hospital ward who die from disease and starvation. She tells me about life after the war, when the men return and there is bread in the bakeries and the shops reopen. She says, Everything will return.

Who could have guessed for fifteen years when Baba and Murat Agha drank tea and raku in our salon, when I kissed Murat Agha's hand as he lay on the cushions, like a polite girl kisses her uncle, that we would live in his house and pay our gold for their

229

troubles just as Baba instructed Mama and Mama instructed me.

When you sleep in the exile's bed linen or drink from his cup do you know his body or his name? Is there no shame in owning our things?

I Have Seen God in the Faces of Men

I have seen God in the mirror and in the faces of men. I have read the poet who is not from this land, this river, this sky or whirling bird or spike leaf. He aroused me and made me his lover, but he did not speak of the horrible, the violent God that I have seen in the mirror and in the faces of men. Did he not see I?

I would like to say: You, when you read this I will buckle below your feet, sprite of wind. You, when you speak my words in your mouth, I will be your grist, your grape leaves, suckling lamb, suckle me. He was assured by his words, but I am a man who has looked into the mirror and I have seen its spectre. My words will not. This is the body that betrays me. I do not hunt for polar bears *or* bivouac *by invading watchfires. This body betrays words.*

> *All this I swallow, it tastes good, I like it well, it*
>   *becomes mine,*
> *I am the man, I suffer'd, I was there.*

I say: I am the man, I suffer; I am here. Here. Why did you never tell me there *is the horrible lie? I am not everywhere,*

231

it is only Here, alone in this attic, in this boy who crouches by the window, a shit a shat, song of myself that only the shitting birds hear and only for the moment I yell out to them. Between the yell into the daylight, it flies up out through the window, it carries onto the air current, electric, who yelled? The boy, the lip, the mind?

Did he wail, Fuck You Cur! The soldiers pricked their ears, they turned a corner and they came again into the house with the old lady. They shoved her, cuffed her, and violated – and the boy upstairs, was it his fingers or his mind read a foreign man's lyric? He heard them or his tympanum detected the soldiers ascending, finding the stairwell in the cupboard behind the dresses and blankets, ascending. Was he Here or There when the soldiers pushed the trap door to the attic open? I sing, Fuck You Cur! Was there any poetry then? Were his agonies a word or vibration, a change of garment, were they language at all?

And in my soul I swear I never will deny him.

I ask you, brother, he does ask the Turkish boy soldiers, Do you have a fag?

Or he asks them, they pull his arms (his arms) behind his back, they beat him around the head and shoulders, blood spills from his ears like water from a cupped rose, What is Reason? He asks them. And what is Love? And what is Life?

No. These are the questions only the poet may ask. A man in his violent stages of death is no maker, but a boy-animal, trussed, shat, spoiled, the horrific meat. He is a sheep or burned dog. Whit-man and Hakan his betrayers Here. None other. No words for the demolition of the man, boy, animal.

He doesn't look at you now from this distance. You cannot

232

see him or find him with your boot heels. He does not see you. Nor Love you.

And to die is different from what anyone supposed. In this sacrifice I do not know what is made holy.

A Sad Ending Again

The town crier walked through the streets announcing the changes.

No town here, notownhere. Move down the hill. There is no town there.

It was not long afterwards that a great flood came, a fire or plague. An earthquake shook the foundations of Kharphert.

No town there, notownthere.

The town became a ruin.

The town crier moved down the hill at a slow pace. He dragged his lame foot along, a new dog followed him and licked his heels. What is my name? the dog barked. Next thing, the town crier said. Tomorrow and not today: no Mezre. Tomorrow and not today: Elazig, our son is born.

Elazig, the dog barked. Elazig! New name in the newworld. What is for dinner?

The town crier walked through the vilayet. From sunup to sundown he walked, dragging his lame foot along and his new dog followed him. In each village the dog barked, What is my name? Not there, not today, not yesterday: there is no village, the town crier announced to the eaves and the cats living below.

They walked and the town crier made a map, yes, yes, yes and no, no, no. He made Xs and taches: this village all right. That one's a goner. Name? Namely, you'll be: Hosköy, Cipköy, Kiyulu, and Yurtbasi.

At the end of his journey his feet ached. His boots had chafed his heels and small toes considerably (but the boots were new and had held up during the long journey overland). This is the nationstate, he said, of my dreams. We speak the same tongue, we use our tongues to lick your cheeks. Welcome, he said, opening his arms wide. Welcome to this newplace. If you don't know it, do not worry. Buy a newmap from the vendor. Ach, the lake is awfully small and timid. You'll see, once it's been enlarged you can bathe in it during the summer months when the heat creeps down your skin like beetles in sweet sugar syrup.

The town crier returned to Elazig and ate a pastry. He licked the crumbs from his fingers and the dog with no name sat at his feet. He reported his progress to his boss.

For a little while, the Commander said, there will be some confusion. The post may be delayed. The cartographers will require overtime and extra pay. But you'll see, it won't take long. Soon the villages will always have existed this way. A few extra dogs. A few extra shoes. Extra women in the haremlik for a few years. Some children who need to work extra hard on their religious training. It's better than dead, it's history.

Who believes the fables and rumours of the djinn against history stories? Soon we'll have tomes of books to elucidate the What Has Always Been True today and yesterday, for two thousand years or more. Elazig, my son. Elazig, today and yesterday. You are the hope and pride of the newnation. What do you say? There has never been another. Türkiye.

The dog stood up on his hind legs as if he were dancing the circle dance. The Commander looked up from his meal of lamb and stuffed cabbage dolma. What's that dog doing here still? he yelled.

Inside, 1917

I am swimming in warm water and thinking about my brothers. The water is clean but clouded, as if someone has stirred the sediment from the lake's floor. I am swimming in water, and black tubes like arms bundle around me, stretching from the floor of the lake to the surface. I can't see the lake's bottom but I know those black arms are rooted there. They ess and sway, underwater cypresses. Soon I am swimming among the bodies. Bodies like the black tubes bundle around me, stretching from the floor of the lake to the surface. There are bodies everywhere I can see. I part them with my hands and fists. They try to close me in. I am looking for my brothers.

I climb the stacks of tonnirs. They stretch towards the sky. There are tonnirs stacked as high as the four-storey school buildings. I run and climb. At the top are half-empty plates of food: pilaf, yogurt soup, kebab. I eat with my hands, I am ravenous.

*   *   *

There is a system in place, like a calendar for the call to prayer. I see the little girl Araxie who was two classes behind me at school. Her black hair hangs loose down her back and she claps her hands together furiously. Haigan's sister, Serpouhy, walks awkwardly with the babe in her belly; Eghis Hanim waves to me from an automobile and her Turkish driver smiles. My classmates skip along; the young scholar they discovered in late autumn hiding in his attic smiles wide; the bootmaker shakes his awl wildly. I don't want to follow them, they walk along together. They ride on horses and ox carts. Everyone moves forward, I know they are going to the lake. I run and climb the stacks of tonnirs. I am enraged, I want to pick up a tonnir and throw it at an open window. A Turkish woman brushes her hair in the window. She smiles at me. Chhhht, I motion to her with my fingers and she backs away from the window. I am afraid she will call the gendarmerie. I am eating from the half-eaten plates of food. Don't let them know I'm here, I motion to her with my hands. I'll kill you. I'll kill you. See this hand? It's shaped like a rifle. Useless, I'll kill you.

I see myself in the glass and my hair is undone. It falls down my back in a silver line.

Anaguil, yavrum. Anaguil, chhhh.
   I lie in the circle of Gülhan Hanim's arms. My sister hugs my legs.
   Yavrum, she says. She rocks me like a babe in her arms. You're dreaming. She brushes my hair from my face, it is still the dark brown I recognize. I turn in her arms and I bury my chin and for the first time since before Mama died I cry in someone's arms. She holds

and breathes softly. She sings the lullaby that Ahmet loves. Anaguil, she says, my baby, chhhh.

It is early morning, the cold is seeping in through the walls. Gülhan Hanim has brought the kerosene lamp. Her arms warm me. In her arms I remember the youngman-scholar they took from the attic near the college. A picture of him stays in my mind. The naked man they pulled onto the streets, his mother screaming behind him. It was in the autumn of that year when things had quieted down for a few weeks. The caravans had long since departed. We thought, now they will leave us alone. Now, we can breathe easier. They dragged him onto the street and in front of the college, which they had made into their barracks, they beat him with their rifle butts. This naked youngman who had shit pressed into his beard and long hair, shit all over his skin and bones body. I remember thinking, is he the last man of our race?

He urinated on their feet and he laughed as they pounded him with their weaponry. The blood flowed down his face. The red and the brown were an awful relief on his pale skin. The youngman-scholar had lost his wits. Do you have a fag? he yelled again and again. His mother pulled her hair and beat her breast. She spoke his name and his name lifted onto the afternoon and rose skyward like a loose cloud. The sun was shining that day; it was a beautiful autumn day in Kharphert. They dragged the youngman into the barracks.

Gülhan Hanim pulled me down another street after Ismet. Don't look, she said. Stop looking.

They left part of that youngman in the town square I later learned. His head on a pike for viewing.

*   *   *

Nevart climbs into my lap and I hold her close. The three of us together on my bedding. In that moment I understand we cannot remain. We must leave this place. I feel my mama's touch, as if she has given me this thought. I must gather my brothers. When this war is finished, we must leave this place.

Rachel's List in Part

Arshanig Eskijian Vergeen Eskijian Missak Eskijian
Vahan Eskijian Hovannes Eskijian Hagop Demirdjian
Yughaper Demirdjian Hratch Demirdjian Nartouhy
Demirdjian Berj Demirdjian Sargis Terzian Melkon
Terzian Shushan Terzian Ohan Terzian Mary Terzian
Oskinaz Terzian Vart Terzian Hamayak Terzian Simon
Terzian Mehmet Mustafa Timur Güneli Meltem Nahit
Ratibe Eduard Basmajian Koharig Basmajian Azniv
Basmajian Lousaper Basmajian Lucine Touryan
Bedros Touryan Krikor Touryan Araxie Touryan Dick-
ran Mariam Hovsep Vahram Hampartzoum Gaspar
Arpine Garo Hoogasian Sara Hoogasian Satenig
Hoogasian Khatoun Hoogasian Eghis Hindlian Harut-
iun Hindlian Krikor Hindlian Bakrat Gregorian Efronia
Gregorian Esther Gregorian Manoug Gregorian Araxie
Gregorian Levon Najarian Hassig Najarian Lisabeth
Najarian Mary Najarian Melane Najarian Elia Parikian
Lucine Parikian Zevart Parikian Hamest Parikian
Armenag Parikian Missak Parikian Parantzem Parikian
Mary Parikian Souren Parikian Setrak Ailanjian Efronia
Ailanjian Hovannes Ailanjian Mariam Ailanjian

Armen Ailanjian Kevork Ailanjian Fevzi Ali Firuz Kamil Gaspar Magdassarian Vart Magdassarian Elmas Magdassarian Arif Hamit Boghos Ignatiosian Arpinee Ignatiosian Hrag Ignatiosian Ohan Ignatiosian Haigan Ignatiosian Serpouhy Tevrizian Artin Tevrizian Anahit Tevrizian Haig Tevrizian Yulia Kazanjian Rachel Eskijian.

Today is Wednesday

Today is Wednesday, the last day for many years that Anaguil sleeps undisturbed. Her sleeping is still a closing of the eyes and a blurred story of blue light and then dawn light and dressing for chores.

She gets up from her sleeping pallet today, she dons her blue dress and she combs and plaits her hair. Nevart sleeps quietly next to her. She gets up and she leaves their bedroom and she walks downstairs to the kitchen where she lights the fire and puts water on to boil. It is dark and still cool inside the house; the coolness before the summer heat begins. She prepares the tea and there is some bread, a hunk of white sheep's cheese, half a cucumber. It is quiet in the house, no one else has risen yet.

She carries the teacup and the small piece of bread and cheese on a copper tray. She walks towards her parents' bedroom. She opens the door, the sunlight is just beginning to stream in through the shuttered windows. There is only a little bit of light, the smallest beams of day pushing past the wooden barriers. She puts the tray down beside the bed and she wonders if she should wake her sleeping mama, her mama who hasn't eaten a full meal in days. She kneels beside the bed and she looks at her mother's sleeping form; her mother curled like a babe, her back towards her, a cut flower, the knees tucked tightly. She thinks she won't wake her mother but will allow her to sleep. She gets up and walks to the door as if to leave; she will go check on her brothers.

What is missing is breath. Her own she can hear loudly as it rains in and out of her mouth. She walks back to her mother's sleeping pallet and she places her hand on the nape of her mother's neck. Her hand a sundered rose.

She would replait her mother's long black hair, it is unkempt and tangled. She would wipe her mother's brow with a cotton cloth damp with orange water blossom. She would lift the bed linen and crawl inside. She would tuck her body around her mother's, hold the body that holds her heart, and rain her breath in and out for the both of them. Here Mama. *I'm here Mama*. In and out. She would never rise from this place. She pulls the bed linen close and she breathes and she closes her eyes as if asleep.

She doesn't know that after today, this Wednesday in June, until many years later in the Lebanon, she will sleep only in small increments and she will learn the hours of dark as well as she knows the times of the day.

There is and there is not

In Beirut, by the sea's edge, I change my name.

My husband when he is not yet my husband laughs and yells, Are you crazy, mademoiselle? But in this I am stubborn. Nevart giggles. It is a topic of uneasy humour and slight awkwardness. My brothers stare at the floor and the sharp corners of the carved wooden chest. Yet I know people can accustom themselves to things much stranger than a name.

I look and look for the girl I was and I can no longer find her. I cannot bear to keep her name. When this name is spoken there is a descent inside of me, a man tipping over a three-storey balustrade.

On 7 June in 1922 – it is a Wednesday – I will go to the photographer's studio for the first time since I was a girl of twelve. I will wear a red silk dress made especially for this occasion. It has a wide collar and pleats darting from the two-finger band around the waist. I will wear the gold filigree necklace Nishan bought for me as a gift, a celebration of his first commercial success. Everything I have on is new. Even my undergarments. I am in my twenties, but you can see in the photograph that I am not a careless young woman. Thick wrinkles make ledges beneath my eyes, like engraved moths' wings. Later in my thirties I will develop the habit of wearing white powder on my face and neck. I cover myself in alabaster powder; I look different in subsequent photographs. Covered up. A ghost.

I look young in 1922 despite the dark circles. In my thirties I begin to age quickly. No one knows how old I am. History and ledgers are in the time Before. I say I don't know my own age, and there are no papers to contradict me. I am thirty-five; I am thirty-two; forty; forty-odd. When I die my daughter says, Maman was born in the old place.

My greatest wish is to have a singing daughter.

I become Venus in Beirut and I sleep soundly. I am becoming her for years. In Garo's Studio on the Rue

245

Dumas I am no longer that other girl. When the camera-man captures the young woman with a too-thick nose who for the first time in seven years wears a new dress and a gold necklace. I also wear shining black-heeled shoes but you cannot see them in the oval photo. My toes hurt. They are lovely bright shoes.

In the time before alabaster facial powder there is a standing young woman in a red silk dress and gold filigree necklace. Her dark hair is pulled behind into a bun at the nape of her neck. She is not a slim woman. She holds her arms behind her back and she stares to the left of the camera lens. The eyes are the centre of the image. They look directly to the left of the camera. Inside there is only blood and nerves, paper, black ink.

There is and there is not the possibility of an auspicious ending.

Arsinee

This is the story rumour writes.

She writes it late at night, while you are dozing.

Don't believe it, she's a liar of the first order. A mendacious tatterdemalion. Rumour prefers rags, piled and layered in untenable positions with rancid colour combinations over tailored suit coats or silk shawls, or pointy tight shoes. She has no shoes to speak of, yes her feet swell and pus. She's always a neonate, lives next door beneath the bridge, at the bottom corner of the well, her back against a stone wall. She ties rags around her head, someone takes a photograph of her and sends it to a foreign country, whereby someone, a well-to-do and sedulous phil-anthropist, sends back a few gold coins in a sealed envelope.

(The sedulous philanthropist, as you may well imagine, is a man, a lazy blue-eyed man in his fifties who lives in the civilized place, who does not play tennis and needs to watch his penchant for salted meats and sweet treats because of obvious protuberant growths (growth rather) that his mistress has warned

247

him do not favour a man of his wealth, stature, etc., and so others will not speak so highly of him perhaps, although he is quite reassured by the tradition which allows him protuberances, mistresses and philanthropy (in that order), in addition to country club admittance, with or without actually swinging the racket on a lawn court. And he can, you know. And the protuberance, by the way and according to rumour, gets in the way of other things protruding, a difficulty at home and hotel alike occasionally.)

Rumour says things like, And so, And so

There was and

There was not

Rumour tells stories; she's a beggar. She lives in Aleppo now. Her name is Arsinee. She's had a difficult life. You may feel sorrow for her – her brother Dickran died beneath an oak on the plains of Anatolia that stretched out for miles. Her mother cast herself into the Euphrates River without word or tug of hand. (Her father?) Shed tears or tug heart or ring your nearest relief agency and send a gold coin or perhaps an old cotton shirt in a sealed envelope. Rumour was five or six when she began. Now she's old and lives with two Kurdish fellows. She lives in Anatolia now. She saw her face on a poster. She doesn't speak Armenian (any more). The Kurdish fellows are old also. Rumour says, I've lived with them since I was eight or nine or ten.

I am telling this story. I ask you, What is esculent? Running toward the dictionary, you answer: you, you, you. We eat her up, a barbecue. Small children are lovely spiked on bayonet tips. Tip for such tipping: throw babes up twisted towards the left eye's view, take into account any wind flows, lift bayonet, straight and fltch! a babe on a bayonet, bayonetbaby. This according to rumour only.

There are a surfeit of rumours. A surfeit of surfeit. Indigent rumours. Spiritual rumours. Fucking rumours. Killer rumours. Bodies. Urine. Schools of orphans. Arsinee often says, And so and so, if you insist too vehemently on any particular particular. Rumour is an evanescent and mendacious tatterdemalion.

Rumour's covenant with her people: I shall not abandon you. A surfeit of surfeit for all time.

This is the story rumour writes.

There are clans who lived on the Anatolian plateau for more than two thousand years. The clans say, We call ourselves *Hai*; call me by my nighest name. Two thousand years is a long time. Long enough to honour the sun and moon, slay the dragon and build a parapet, castle and a monastery in Ani. Long enough to riddle the land with khatchk'ars – asserting in stone crosses the multitude. Long enough to fertilize the earth with bones. To raise a few dogs and sheep, slap the mule's hindquarters. To make buttery pilaf and pound the meat until it is tender. Weave the kilim and embroider the rosette. Arsinee traces her roots back two thousand years or more, to her grandmother, the first woman, for rumour's sake we call her Eva, who liked apricots more than apples and did not wear shoes and loved to twist her foot from side to side, lift her leg and admire her talus – she had no word in Armenian or Hebrew or Greek for that beautiful protuberance at the base of her leg. A rise in the skin, a bone-hill. The word came later.

These people like to tell jokes, stories, fables and sing quite a bit. Fond of lamentations. They construct edifices from Constantinople to Yerevan. They plough and sew. Delicate lace pillowcases and a marriage veil. There is language; they point at things and say: this and this and this. Haik is my father and Noah is my father, and I remember in the second month on the twenty-seventh day how the earth was dry, we played in the sunlight for hours. We have built villages. We purchased a new bell from Massachusetts for our church. We played the organ. We pounded the spices for basturma and made the sujuk for the winter months. We cured a chest cold with a bit of hollyhock flower boiled into a tea. We shaved our beards and buried gold coins, treatises, books of poetry. We buried mounds of gold coins, rumour has it; rumour says they hunted for years in our villages and quarters, they dug up the foundations and orchards in search of the treasure.

When I was born I had no ideas. That I would tie rags around my head and later on my feet; I lost my shoes or they were stolen from me. I walked to Der-el-Zor with my brother and my mama and aunties and cousins towards Arabia. I didn't know that they would disappear in the rivers and beneath the trees and by the roadside, on the marauding horseback, or that they wouldn't be there at all, And so, And so. A mendacious tatterdemalion? Evanescent? I'm a girl, Arsinee. This is the story that I write, rumour writes this story. She writes it late at night, while you are dozing. I've seen my yellowed photograph on posters and in a periodical. I've seen the games that gendarmes play with their weaponry and babes. I am always a neonate, when you say my name or talk about me. I am old also. I don't speak Armenian (any more). I live with two Kurdish fellows in the village of Tadim. They are old men. I've lived with them since I was eight or nine or ten. I have no children. Rumour is barren.

Don't believe it; she's a liar of the first order. A mendacious tatterdemalion.

My Darlings

When she thinks of herself she imagines herself walking along the narrow streets endlessly, stopping at the places that have views of the Anatolian plains which stretch beyond the town and on a clear morning in spring allow her to see Mezre and sometimes even the neighbouring Armenian village, Hoolakeuy. And as she walks her shod feet hit the cobbled stones or the hard-packed dirt and the sound reverberates inside her and reminds her of the hollow whack that summer melons make as women snap their fingers against the skins to check for ripeness; and she is always there now, a solitary walker with her head bent and covered in a çarsaf and moving toward an unknown destination. In her mind she will walk to the west end of Kharphert and take the hidden trail down to Mezre and sneak into the town and drift by the bazaar, down Ambar Mahallesi Street to the American Consul's house, behind the XI Army Corps barracks, and Vali Sabit Bey's walled gardens. She will skirt the deserted orphanage of the Capuçin monks and Mosque numbers one, two, three and four; she will weave in and out of the Armenian quarter, the Muslim quarter, the rich three-storey neighbourhoods and the poor one-storey back alleyways; she will speak to no one and she will come to the edge of the town and head towards the villages. She will cast her feet toward Hoolakeuy in search of their famous cheese and butter and upon arriving she will imagine herself buying hot bread and slathering butter on it. But as she nears Hoolakeuy she sees that it lies empty and only the wind occupies the eaves; only cats live in the houses that are no longer houses but half burned and cleared of wood (they took it for the previous winter) falling-down mudbrick piles, and she imagines that she continues walking out of Hoolakeuy towards Bozmashen and Yegheki and when she approaches these towns she finds again only cats and missing wooden doors and windows and so she continues for weeks passing Huseinik and Haboosi and Kesserik and Susury and Pertag or the places where they had been one year and nine months before. They have changed geography, she thinks. And she continues until she reaches the Der-el-Zor and she stops at all of the streams and she drinks the water; she does not take a circuitous route to Aleppo. When she arrives at the edges of Beirut she smells the sea air which she has always dreamed of so that her shod feet take her down to the boardwalk and she walks along the waterfront, breathing deeply, and she stops and buys a pastry from a corner vendor and she takes off the çarsaf and she gathers her brothers and blue-eyed Nevart close to her and she says, My darlings, new spring has arrived, and she began to sing this song.

Glossary

All spellings of the words listed below are my own choice of transliterations of the original Armenian and Turkish. The designations of Armenian and Turkish are in some cases fluid as one would expect in a multi-lingual society.

A=Armenian
T=Turkish

agha (T) – lord, master
aman (T) – oh, literally means 'mercy'
Amerigatsi (A) – American
amo (A) – uncle
amot (A) – shame
an-ne (T) – mother
anoushig (A) – pretty
baba (A/T) – father
bey (T) – mister, a gentleman
çarsaf (T) – veil
Der Hyre (A) – Orthodox Apostolic priest
dev (T) – giant

digin (A) – Mrs

dilek (T) – a woman's first name, meaning 'wish'

djinn (T/A) – evil spirits, ghosts

duduk (A) – reed instrument

eench (A) – what

eench-eh? (A) – what's the matter?

eench-spesez? (A) – how are you?

effendi (T) – sir

gâvur (T) – infidel, nonbeliever

gendarme (T) – policeman

hai (A) – Armenian

hamam (T) – bathhouse

hanim (T) – lady, Mrs

hayrig (A) – father

hokees (A) – my soul

iyo (A) – yes

kaimakam (T) – police chief

khatchk'ar (A) – stone cross

kifteh (A) – usually a meat dish made with wheat bulgur

kna (A) – go

la-vem (A) – fine

mairig (A) – mother

mardiros (A) – a man's first name, meaning 'martyr'

meydan (T) – commissary, townhall, town jail

millet (T) – community; non-Muslim groups within
    the Ottoman Empire

nene (A) – grandmother

raku (T) – alcoholic beverage

shud (A) – hurry

tahn (A) – a yogurt drink

tonnir (A) – henter

tourshi (A) – pickles

vali (T) – governor

vilayet (T) – province

voch (A) – no
yavrum (T) – my baby
yegu (A) – come
zocanch (A) – mother-in-law

Acknowledgements

Although this novel is a work of fiction, some of the places, characters, and events depicted are based in historical fact. The twin towns of Kharphert and Mezre existed during Ottoman times, each with substantial Armenian communities. The characters of Hagop, Yughaper, Anaguil, Nevart, Nishan, Stepan and Jirair Demirdjian, as well as Consul Leslie Davis, are inspired by real historical figures, although their portraits in the novel are fictional. During World War 1, the Armenian communities from both towns, as in the rest of Anatolia, were massacred and deported leading to the permanent removal of the Armenian presence in the area.

Many of the texts I read in the course of my research had a profound impact on the writing of the book. In particular, the first person accounts and memoirs by surviving Ottoman Armenians were invaluable. John Minassian's book, *Many Hills Yet to Climb*, opened up the world of Anatolia and relayed his experience during the genocide with pathos, reflection, and dignity; I am deeply indebted. Also significant were *Vergeen A*

258

Survivor of the Armenian Genocide by Mae M. Derdarian and *Days of Tragedy in Armenia: Personal Experiences in Harpoot, 1915–1917* by Henry H. Riggs. *The Slaughterhouse Province*, which contains US Consul Leslie Davis' report to the Consular Agency regarding the years 1914–1917, was extraordinary. Davis' reports which appear in the novel are quoted from the official dispatches Davis wrote during that period. The Official Proclamation on page 120 was also reprinted from the appendix of *The Slaughterhouse Province*; originally it was an enclosure to a dispatch from the US Consul at Trebizond to the US Embassy in Constantinople. I thank Aristide D. Caratzas, Publisher, for their permission to reprint the material here. Ronald Grigor Suny's book *Looking Toward Ararat* was very helpful as were Donald E. Miller and Lorna Touryan Miller's *Survivors An Oral History of the Armenian Genocide* and then US ambassador to Turkey Henry Morgenthau's book, *Ambassador Morgenthau's Story*. There are a number of lines taken from Walt Whitman's "Song of Myself" in the sections depicting the character Sargis Terzian including pages 47, 50, 51 and 231–233.

Many people were instrumental in the writing of this novel, however indirectly or directly. I would like to thank Elmaz Abinader for giving me the first welcome into the MFA program at Mills College; Maxine Hong Kingston and Cristina Garcia for their guidance; my peerless writing peers for continual support; Minh-Ha Pham and Daniel Fishman for coming over at a moment's notice and helping to find order in chaos; Tamara Guirado for all those titles; Frances Sackett from the beginning for reading and always loving the reading; and most especially to Ginu Kamani for the inspiration, the edges and finally, for helping to make the contacts. I thank Romeo Garcia, Sharon Nesbitt and the rest of the staff and the students of Mills College Upward Bound for the time and support and the questions of origin. Gia Aivazian, librarian at the Armenian and Greek Research Library of UCLA, who patiently answered many questions via e-mail. Peter Balakian for taking the time to read the manuscript. I am indebted.

A special thanks to Sandra Dijkstra for her belief in the book and for supporting it through the process. Thanks also to Susan Watt for her diligent care of this novel.

I am very thankful to my family for their continuous faith: Dad and Janice; Miroquer Nevart who doesn't want to remember and who still speaks with our ghosts each day in the garden; David, amor, who always said Yes and Yes, when it wasn't practical and who listened many evenings to the latest instalment. And finally, to Mama—you hold my heart in your hand. This is your book. Thank you.